Enid Blyton

The Secret Valley

by
T. J. Bolton

For further information on Enid Blyton please visit *www.blyton.com*

With thanks to Tony Summerfield,
organiser of the Enid Blyton Society,
and Anita Bensoussane for
their encouragement

Hardback ISBN 978-1-84135-753-9
Paperback ISBN 978-1-84135-678-5

Illustrated by Val Biro

First published 2009 by Award Publications Limited

Published by Award Publications Limited,
The Old Riding School, The Welbeck Estate,
Worksop, Nottinghamshire, S80 3LR

Hardback 09 1
Paperback 12 3

Printed in the United Kingdom

Contents

Return to Baronia

"Look! Mountains everywhere! You can see them peeping through the breaks in the cloud!" yelled Nora, turning round to her brother, Mike, sitting behind her in the small aeroplane.

"That probably means we're over Baronia at last," replied Mike looking and feeling excited. He called to the pilot. "How much longer, Pilescu?"

There was no reply from the big red-haired man seated at the controls of the sleek silver and blue aeroplane. His smart uniform was also silver and blue, the national colours of his country, Baronia. Wearing headphones, he was busy talking into a microphone in his own language while glancing at the various dials in front of him.

"It's no use, he can't hear you," said Mike's older sister, Peggy, seated beside Nora. "Listen, he's speaking in Baronian so we can't have much further to... help! Whatever's happening? My tummy's going all funny."

"We're starting to descend, silly!" laughed Jack, his mischievous blue eyes gleaming. He turned to Mike who was next to him. "I think this answers your question, Mike. It won't be long before we land. But Peggy's right. It does sort of turn your tummy over going down."

Mike and Nora Arnold were twins and very much

alike, although Nora was a bit smaller than her brother.
They had black, curly hair and dark eyes just like their
mother. In contrast, their sister Peggy, who was a year
older, had blond hair and blue eyes.

Once, when their parents had flown to Australia in
their little plane, the White Swallow, Mike, Peggy and
Nora had stayed on a farm with their Aunt Harriet and
Uncle Henry. Unfortunately, the White Swallow came
down on a desert island and, when it seemed that the
Arnolds would not return, the uncle and aunt treated
the children very badly. They were forced to work for
hours on end on the farm and never taken anywhere.

Jack, an orphan, living nearby with his grandfather,
also had to work most of the time and had no friends
apart from the Arnold children. Although he was clearly
older than Mike, he sadly didn't know his exact age. An
intelligent boy, he knew the names of all the flowers,

trees and birds, and how to survive out of doors in all weather. When, eventually, the four children felt they had endured enough from the uncaring grown-ups, they decided to run away to a secret island in the middle of Lake Wildwater. There they survived for many months under Jack's leadership until, to their huge surprise and delight, Captain and Mrs Arnold were found. On returning home and hearing about Jack's plight, the Arnolds welcomed him into their family and treated him like another son.

Now the four children were on their way to Baronia, a mountainous kingdom, where their parents were going to test a new small plane. Captain and Mrs Arnold had flown to Baronia earlier in the White Swallow, which was too small to accommodate the entire family, although the children's luggage was stowed on board.

"I wonder if Pilescu will collect Paul tonight or wait

until the morning," said Mike. "Hopefully he'll come tonight so we can all be together straight away."

"I do hope so," said Nora. "You boys are with him at school all the time but Peggy and I haven't seen him for ages. You know, I still can't believe we rescued a real prince when we stayed at the Peep-Hole."

Paul really was a prince. When his father, the King of Baronia, had been very ill, Paul had been kidnapped and hidden in an old house in the tiny hamlet of Spiggy Holes in Cornwall where the other four children were staying. They had managed to rescue him and hide on their secret island until the enemy found out where they were and they returned to the Peep-Hole. Unknown to them, Paul's father had regained his health and was well enough to travel to Spiggy Holes in person to fetch his son and thank the rescuers. Since then, the four children and Prince Paul had become firm friends, sharing many more adventures, one being in Baronia itself.

Travelling in Paul's plane with his pilot, they were about to land in Baronia again. Looking through the windows, the children were surprised to still see nothing but mountains below even though they were rapidly descending.

"Surely we can't land here, Pilescu?" remarked Jack, noticing that the pilot had stopped talking into his microphone and was looking intently through the windscreen.

The burly Baronian with his flaming red beard turned slightly. "Don't you worry, we're approaching the test ground, which is in a large valley," he shouted. "It's almost entirely surrounded by these mountains

– that is why it was chosen. Now, hold tight. We'll be going down very steeply in a moment."

The words had scarcely left his mouth when the plane tilted forwards and began a steep descent. The children gasped as they saw the craggy mountain range drop steeply down into the valley below where there was plenty of greenery and, to one side, a large lake. The plane circled the lake and landed bumpily on a flat stretch of ground between it and the mountains. Nearby were two log cabins.

"Now you can unfasten your belts and leave your seats," said Pilescu once the plane had come to a halt. He rose to open the door and let down the steps before turning to the children. "Welcome once again to Baronia."

"It's smashing to be back here," said Jack, leaping down to the ground. Another aeroplane a short distance away caught his attention. "Look, there's the White Swallow."

"And here come Mummy and Daddy," Peggy pointed out, seeing her parents approaching from one of the cabins. "And just look at those lovely log cabins."

"This is a strange testing ground," said Mike as he greeted his parents. He looked around in surprise. Apart from the cabins, there were no buildings and, other than the two planes, no aircraft to test. "I expected to see hangars and offices, not to mention aeroplanes."

"You didn't think you'd be staying in the test area, did you?" laughed Captain Arnold. "It's down there at the other end of the valley, way beyond the lake. You'll be staying here with Paul's man, Pilescu, and I expect

Ranni will be joining you before too long. You'll be glad you're away from all the noise and the hustle and bustle. Mummy and I will fly down to the base in the White Swallow once you are settled in."

"I've already sorted out your cases so you won't have horrible unpacking to do," added Mrs Arnold. "So come along into your cabin. There's a meal prepared, as I expect you're all hungry. You will join us, I hope, Pilescu? We've set a place for you."

"I will be pleased to join you, thank you, then I must fly to the palace," Pilescu replied solemnly, giving a slight bow. "I will return in the morning with our little prince."

"Won't you be coming back with him tonight?" asked Nora sounding disappointed.

"Darkness falls here very suddenly," explained Pilescu. "It's difficult enough landing here in daylight because of the mountains and the lake, not to mention all the rocks and boulders you see scattered about all over the place. Landing at night with the Prince of Baronia on board is out of the question. You will see our little prince quite early tomorrow, I promise you."

The Arnolds led the way into the log cabin where a large meal was laid out on a table on the veranda. It was not long before everyone was tucking in and chatting excitedly.

"Are these the Killimooin Mountains?" asked Nora remembering the adventure they had had in the mountains and in the secret forest.

"Oh no," replied Pilescu shaking his head. "The Killimooins are further east and form a circle around the secret forest, remember, but these mountains are just like them. They are rough and very steep near the top. The only open pass into this valley is near the test ground so tough road vehicles are able to enter and leave."

"Can't people come through the pass and spy on the test site?" asked Jack, surprised.

"Certainly not," said Captain Arnold. "There is a permanent guard at the head of the pass. Nobody is allowed through without a permit and no plane is allowed to land without permission. There's a track running right round the valley which is regularly patrolled by a Jeep. You'll see it from time to time."

"You'll have the mountainside, the lake and little island all to yourselves," said Mrs Arnold smiling. "It's apparently quite safe to swim in the lake but, I warn you now, the water can be cold, especially in the morning. Mind you, it will feel most welcome and refreshing when the hot Baronian sun is overhead."

"I remember the heat from last time we were here," remarked Jack. He leant over the veranda rail and craned his neck to see the mountains behind the cabin and addressed Pilescu. "What's on the other side of the mountains behind us? More mountains?"

"Beyond these mountains is a steep drop down to the River Jollu," explained Pilescu. "The mountains are so sheer that only properly equipped mountaineers can traverse them. To the right, the range continues towards Killimooin while, over the other side of the valley where those rugged hills are, there used to be a pass into a fairly small valley. A torrential rainstorm caused landslides which completely blocked this pass and the one at the other end of that valley. Luckily there was nobody living there any more as rocks and boulders had previously fallen from the mountains making farming almost impossible. Now it's completely isolated – a secret valley really – as there's insufficient space for a plane to land. And beyond is Maldonia, a country whose government is not always friendly towards us."

At first, the children looked at each other alarmed on hearing that Baronia's neighbour was not always friendly, but they soon forgot about it as they enjoyed their food. Once the meal was over, Pilescu consulted his watch and, after thanking the Arnolds for the meal, strode over to the blue and silver plane, followed by the four children.

"Goodbye for now," he said as he clambered aboard. "I will see you again in the morning."

"Come as early as you can," called Peggy. "We want to see Paul again, then we can explore all around here together."

Suddenly the plane's engines sprang into life. Pilescu slowly taxied the aircraft round then, waving from the cockpit, bumped along the makeshift runway before lifting off and flying steeply upwards and disappearing over the mountains.

"Let's have a look at our rooms," suggested Jack as they returned to the cabin. "I'm glad we haven't got any unpacking to do. I hate packing and unpacking."

Two wings were attached to the sitting and dining area of the cabin at opposite ends. In one wing were two bedrooms, in the other, three bedrooms. This was where the children were to sleep.

"Paul will have a room to himself with a phone communicating with Pilescu," pointed out Captain Arnold. "The other two rooms this end are for the rest of you. Mummy and I will be sleeping in the cabin next door when we come to this end of the valley, although while we're actually testing, we'll have accommodation near the test ground."

"Will you fly up and down the valley in the White Swallow?" asked Nora.

"Oh no," replied her mother. "We'll obviously fly down tomorrow but we've been informed we can use a Jeep when we're travelling in the valley itself. As Pilescu said, there's a track going right round the foot of the mountains."

"Shall we start exploring outside?" suggested Peggy looking out of a window.

"Let's just go down to the lake and leave proper exploring until Paul arrives," answered Jack. "It'll be more fun when all five of us are together."

"I'd *love* to see that hidden valley Pilescu mentioned," said Mike, thinking back to their earlier conversation. "It sounds mysterious and exciting."

"Well, you can't," said Captain Arnold. "You heard what Pilescu said. It's completely encircled by mountains since the two ways in and out became blocked after that storm. It's just deserted now – almost a secret."

"I like the sound of that," said Jack staring out across the lake to the mountains beyond. "A secret valley – and to think it's just over those mountains!"

Together Once More

Next morning, after a hearty breakfast, the children decided to wander down to the lake to await the arrival of Prince Paul. The sun was already peering over the rugged mountains, casting its warm rays down into the valley.

"Mind you keep well clear of the runway when you hear Pilescu's plane approaching," warned Captain Arnold as they went outside. "Once Paul is safely settled in, your Mother and I will fly down to the base as we're due to start testing this very morning."

"Can't you tell us *anything* about the new plane now that we're here?" begged Mike, his head on one side. "After all, we can only tell Pilescu and Paul, and I bet they both know about the plane already."

"I suppose there's no harm telling you something now," replied Mrs Arnold looking at her husband. "It's a small plane – the clever thing about it is that it hardly needs any runway space to take off and land. It can land on fairly bumpy ground like just here. And it is able to make sharp turns – very useful in wild and rugged countries like Baronia. Daddy and I have been invited to evaluate it alongside Baronia's own test pilots."

"Listen, I can hear the sound of engines coming up the valley," interrupted Nora listening intently. "Is that the secret plane?"

"I doubt it," said Captain Arnold with a laugh. "There are plenty of tests taking place down there, many involving engines. It can get quite hectic."

"Well, I'm glad we're this end of the valley," said Peggy. "It would be awful having to put up with that noise all day long. Now I understand why these two cabins have been built up here. A sort of escape. It'll be fun exploring this end of the valley."

"We've been told to warn you to keep off the dangerous ledges on the higher parts of the mountains on this side of the valley," said Mrs Arnold. "So stay on the lower sections where it's quite safe as long as you're careful."

"And don't play on the landslide on the other side of the valley," added Captain Arnold sternly.

"We'll be careful," promised Jack, who was a responsible boy. He scoured the cloudless sky for any sign of an aircraft but not one was to be seen. "I hope Pilescu won't be long. I want to go exploring and perhaps have a swim if it gets any hotter. Come on, you three. I thought we were going down to the lake."

It certainly was becoming quite hot so the thought of a swim later on was very appealing. Watched by their parents, the four hastily crossed the runway and then dodged between boulders, some quite large, as they made their way to the lake with its sparkling, rippling blue water reflecting the sunshine and the cornflower-blue sky. Further down the lake and not far out from the shore was a small island which seemed to be covered with trees.

"It reminds me of our secret island," remarked Nora, pointing.

"Our secret island is much bigger than *that* island!" exclaimed Jack with a laugh. "Still, it will be good fun to row out to it. I can see a couple of rowing boats tethered to what looks like a little jetty. I presume they are for us to use. We could swim out to it, for that matter."

Beside the lake, the four perched on flat-topped boulders as they waited for Paul's plane to appear. All the time there was the distant drone of engines from the far end of the valley. On occasions, the drone became a crescendo before dying away altogether. It all seemed so out of place in such a peaceful and idyllic scene.

"Look at all these butterflies," said Mike, fascinated by the little creatures fluttering about and landing on the various shrubs and flowers. "What lovely bright colours. Just like some of the birds I've seen."

"I expect they sensibly keep to this end of the valley," said Peggy, also watching them. Then she glanced across the lake. "You know, I should think we could easily walk right round this lake. Mind you, there must be a stream leading out of it so we might not be able to cross it. I wonder where it is."

"Hidden by the island, I expect," said Jack. "We might be able to wade across it…"

"Listen, there's a different aeroplane sound," interrupted Nora, gazing into the sky. "It's not coming from down the valley but somewhere over the mountains opposite."

"It's Paul's plane!" yelled Mike, spotting the sleek blue and silver aircraft skimming the mountain tops before swooping steeply down into the valley. Just as it did yesterday, the plane circled the lake then came to a

halt on the runway near the cabins.

The children leapt down off their boulders and ran towards the runway. The plane's door was opened, the steps lowered, and there was Prince Paul, beaming with delight to see his friends again. He hugged the girls and asked them how they were as he had not seen them for some time. He had, of course, been with the boys recently at school.

"Welcome again to my lovely country," he said looking around. "Have you had time to explore yet? It's very wild up here, and very, very beautiful."

"No, we've been no further than the lake," replied Jack. "We waited for you so we could all explore together. Oh, hello again, Pilescu. Is Ranni with you?"

"He'll be along in a few days," replied the Baronian, coming down the steps with Paul's bag. "He is to fly the King to Jonnalongay in the south of Baronia in a day or two to attend to some matters of government."

By now, Captain and Mrs Arnold had appeared from their cabin and came to welcome the little prince. "It seems strange to welcome you to the cabin as it's in your own country, Paul," laughed Mrs Arnold. "It's lovely to see you again. How are your parents?"

"Very well thank you, Mrs Arnold," replied Paul politely, giving a slight bow to her and Captain Arnold, his manners, as always, impeccable. "I shall enjoy being here. In the palace grounds I have to be so dignified but here I can be just like your children, my friends. I can run around in shirt and shorts instead of my princely Baronian costume."

"Come on, we'll show you your room," called Mike running over to the lodge. "We've got one part of this cabin to ourselves. Pilescu will be at the other end, and so will Ranni when he comes."

"But you have a phone that will link you to me immediately, my little lord," stated Pilescu at once. "And it will link you by radio to the Palace."

"Well I won't use it very often," declared Paul, hurriedly following Mike. "I want to be away from the palace and telephones. I just want to be free like you."

Everyone went inside the cabin. Pilescu unpacked Paul's bag, putting the contents neatly into the cupboards and drawers while Paul explored every room. Then Captain and Mrs Arnold said it was time they flew down to the test area now that Pilescu was in charge of the children.

"Can we come down to the test ground some time?" asked Mike, curious to see what was going on.

"We might be able to arrange it, but I cannot promise," replied Captain Arnold.

"I could arrange it if I wanted to," announced Paul haughtily, putting on his serious, princely look. Then he smiled. "But I would rather nobody knows I am here otherwise I would have to have several bodyguards watching me every minute of the day. I want to be like you four."

"So, come on, let's go outside and explore," suggested Nora. "We'll just see Mummy and Daddy off first."

While Pilescu walked to the blue and silver Baronian plane to move it off the runway, Captain and Mrs Arnold went over to the White Swallow and started up the engines. The plane bumped along the grass and onto the firm runway and, with a roar, flew up over the lake and down the valley.

"Let's go down towards that island," said Paul. Then he put his head on one side as a thought occurred to him. "Wait, I'll just go and fetch some chocolate for us to eat as we explore."

"Smashing!" declared Jack. "I do like Baronian chocolate. Its always tastes of honey and cream."

Paul soon reappeared from the cabin with bars of delicious chocolate for everyone. Pilescu watched them make their way down to the lake, not really wanting to let the prince, whom he had held when just a few minutes old, out of his sight.

The five children walked along the shore, looking at what seemed to be little waves dancing towards them, making soothing lapping sounds. Having come off the surrounding mountains, the water was perfectly pure and clear. Soon the children had passed the start of the runway and were opposite the island, which was bigger than it had seemed to be from the cabins. It was mainly covered with trees, but a flat area with mooring posts was visible to one side from which a path led into the little wood.

"We could easily swim out to the island," said Jack. "I hope you've brought your swimming costume, Paul."

"Of course, but we'll row out there first," decided Paul. Kneeling down, he put a hand in the water and let out a yell. "This water's ever so cold. We can't swim in it. We'd freeze!"

Everyone laughed at the expression on Paul's face. "Mummy said the water would be cold," said Peggy remembering her Mother's words. "But I expect we'll appreciate it if it gets really hot."

"There's a stream down there leading into the lake," said Mike, "and a bridge over it – I suppose that's for the patrol Jeep Daddy mentioned."

"And look, the stream comes from that waterfall over there near the foot of the mountains!" exclaimed Nora in delight. "Do let's go over to it. I love the sound of waterfalls. I suppose we can't hear it from here because of the droning noise from the other end of the valley."

"Let's follow the stream all the way back to the waterfall," shouted Paul running on ahead. "I'll race you to it."

Despite his lead, Paul was easily overtaken by Jack who reached the meandering stream first. It was not very deep, but was flowing fairly swiftly. In it were many large stones, some of them flat and close together.

Jack jumped from one to another and was soon on the other side.

"We don't need to use the bridge to cross the stream," he called to the others. "We can use the stepping stones. Come across. The waterfall looks easier to reach this side."

One by one they carefully crossed the stream using the stones. Paul had almost reached the other side when he unfortunately missed his footing and ended up with one foot in the water.

"Brrr, It's cold like the lake!" he cried out, screwing up his face while the others looked on with huge grins. "Now I'll have to put up with a wet foot. It's a good job Pilescu didn't see what happened or he would run over here and take me back to the cabin to dry out."

"Your foot will dry in no time in the heat," said Mike. He turned towards the mountain towering ahead. "Well, we've crossed the stream. Now for the waterfall!"

The Waterfall and the Lake

Chatting away, the children followed the twisting, singing stream to the foot of a magnificent waterfall near the base of the mountain. The roaring water tumbled from a great height directly into a foaming pool in the rocks some way above their heads, sending huge splashes and fine spray in every direction. It spilled over the side of the rocks to cascade down in a variety of small, frothy falls, to eventually form the gurgling stream.

"Isn't the spray refreshing?" shouted Peggy, licking her lips. She looked slyly at Paul, a short distance away. "It's lovely and cold, just like the stream and the lake."

Paul gave a grin as he was now used to being teased, taking it in good part. "I expect it is wild and rough on top like most of my country's mountains," he said. "The River Jollu is on the other side of this one but I do not know what is behind the ones over there."

"Ah, but *we* do," answered Mike mysteriously. "The Secret Valley!"

Paul looked in surprise. "The Secret Valley!" he exclaimed. "The test ground is at the end of *this* valley so *this* is the secret one."

"Pilescu told us there used to be a pass from this valley into the one on the other side of those mountains, but it was blocked by huge landslides after a terrific storm," explained Jack.

"And the same thing happened at the other end, so no-one can enter it from Maldonia," added Nora. "It's more of a secret valley than this one."

"Of course, Maldonia!" exclaimed Paul, his eyes ablaze. "My father, the King, says the Maldonians are also trying to build a new type of plane. They aren't very pleased that our plane is much more advanced than theirs. It can do things theirs can't. But I like the sound of a secret valley. There are lots of hidden, wild places in Baronia. Do you remember the Secret Forest last time you were here?"

"And the adventure with the robbers," said Mike thinking back. "That was very exciting."

"This waterfall reminds me of the time when Mafumu and I discovered a way into the Secret Mountain behind a fall," recalled Jack. "We'll need to climb higher to find if there's a way into the mountain behind this one."

"There's a way up here," called Peggy, moving back a little. "We could climb up these rocks on the right to that ledge up there. It's not so close to the waterfall that we'd be soaked but, as it's higher, it should give us a great view of it."

Jack immediately leapt up as agile as a mountain goat. The others followed, taking care where the misty spray had made the stones slippery. Every so often they gave little yells as the breeze blew icy cold spray into their faces. Soon they were on the large, flat slab looking down to where the main fall plunged into a huge, hollowed out rock, frothing and foaming like a witch's cauldron. The noise was now almost deafening, so the children had to shout to make themselves heard.

"There is no way into the mountain behind this waterfall," yelled Paul sounding disappointed as he pointed to the sheer cliff behind the tumbling water. It was obvious to the children that attempting to even approach the fall would be dangerous due to the wet, slimy, jagged rocks all round.

"You were right, Peggy," shouted Nora turning to gaze across the valley. "There *is* a little river running out of the lake. Oh look! There's a Jeep stopping near our cabin."

"There's the airbase in the distance," observed Mike. "I'm glad we can't hear engines screeching. The sound of the falling water is much more pleasant."

"Being next to it is a bit too noisy for me," declared Jack. "I've an idea. How about asking Pilescu for a picnic lunch to take to the island? It's getting quite hot so we could have a swim while we're there."

"Sounds super," said Peggy as everyone, including Paul, agreed. She glanced down at the stream and sighed. "Climbing down is going to be more difficult than climbing up."

"That's because you can't always see where to put your feet going down," explained Jack. "Don't worry, *I'll* go first." He cautiously lowered himself on to a ledge but this led to a steep drop so he had to scramble back, wiping spray from his face. "I thought we came up just there. I'll try further along. Ah, I remember climbing round that granite tipped rock."

Once again he carefully dropped between two huge boulders and, this time, saw more rocks leading down to the base of the waterfall. Noticing footholds he called the others. "Come down here, but don't let go of handholds until your feet are firmly placed. It's quite easy lower down, as the stones are like steps. But watch out, as some of them are slippery."

Slowly they descended to the floor of the valley, the din from the waterfall fading somewhat even though it was just above them. Reaching the stream, Paul wisely let Jack take the lead. "I don't want to get a wet foot again," he grinned, "especially as Pilescu is watching. If he sees me fall he will come immediately. Come on, we will ask him for a picnic."

As the children approached, they were dismayed to find the Baronian looking grim. He almost had to force himself to smile as they hurried up to him.

"Whatever is the matter, Pilescu?" asked Paul earnestly. "Have we done something wrong?"

"No, no, of course not, my little prince," was the immediate reply. "Kyril and Fredrik called in the Jeep and have informed me that certain plans referring to the new plane are missing."

"Do you mean they've been stolen or simply can't be found?" asked Peggy.

"It seems they were removed from a file yesterday or the day before," replied Pilescu. "Your parents were being shown some documents when it became obvious that certain pages were missing."

"How can anybody come into this valley and leave without being seen?" demanded Paul.

"There are guards at the entrance and guards keeping watch from the mountainside," said Pilescu. "Nobody can come into the valley undetected, even at night."

"So the plans must still be in the valley," said Jack, his

head on one side.

"They will be well hidden until they can be smuggled away," said Pilescu. "It is very serious. Very serious indeed. But, tell me, why were you rushing to me?"

Speaking at once, the children told Pilescu of their idea of having a picnic lunch on the island instead of in the cabin. He relaxed and smiled down at them.

"I understand what you want even though you all speak at once," he said nodding his head. "This is a good idea of yours. Come inside the cabin and I'll show you what I intended us to have for lunch. You can pack it in a basket or two and take the picnic hamper from the kitchen. Don't forget to take plenty to drink as it's becoming very hot."

"Good, there's plenty to eat," said Paul once they were inside the cabin. "I really feel hungry after all our exercise. Guess where we went, Pilescu? Right up to the waterfall! It was so, so noisy where it fell into a pool and the spray made us very wet."

"You went to the waterfall!" exclaimed Pilescu. "You must be careful my little lord. It's very dangerous by a waterfall. The rocks become so slippery."

"Oh, we're used to exploring," said Jack putting bottles of fizzy drink into a basket. "But we did take care, Pilescu. We didn't climb on wet rocks."

Pilescu smiled, but could not help worrying about his little prince even though he knew the other four children always kept a watchful eye on him. Soon the basket was full. The children put on their swimming costumes under their clothes before setting off for the lake. Once in the boat, Jack took the oars after showing Paul how to untie the mooring rope.

It was a delightful picnic on the little island. Across the lake was a backdrop of steep hills and mountains, some of which had waterfalls tumbling down them like the one they had visited earlier. It was now becoming very hot and soon, to the accompaniment of the lapping water, the children nodded off, one by one, in the shelter of the trees.

An insect buzzing round her face made Peggy wake first, wondering where on earth she was. For a moment, she even thought she was on the secret island, then realised that she and the others were indeed on an island, but in Baronia.

"The exercise and the meal have made us all sleepy," she muttered to herself, standing up. "Now shall I wake the others or jump in the lake for a swim?"

But before she could do either, the sound of her movements made the other four open their eyes and look around as they too wondered where they were.

"Fancy us dropping off to sleep!" exclaimed Jack looking at his watch. "How annoying. Well, we've slept for some time so it'll be safe to have a good swim to wake ourselves up."

Soon the five children were splashing about in the clear water. They all yelled when they first jumped in because it was so cold, but it was just what they needed under the hot Baronian sun. Even Paul enjoyed it although he had shivered violently at first. Jack was the best swimmer. The others, especially Paul, watched in admiration as he dived and swam under water some distance away from the island. Then he popped his head up and swam back.

"There are some brightly coloured fish in this lake," he called, pausing to take deep breaths. "They don't look anything like the ones around our Secret Island."

"In Baronia, there are—" began Paul, but he was interrupted by the others.

"...the best fish in the world!" they yelled, broad grins across their faces.

"How can you know what I intended to say?" asked Paul, looking surprised.

"Because you always say that Baronia has the best of everything," replied Peggy.

"That is because I am very proud of my country," said Paul solemnly, using his princely voice. "And you should be proud of yours, too. But you are wrong because I was going to say there are colourful fish in all the Baronian mountain lakes. It is strange how the water feels quite warm now but it was freezing when we jumped in."

"We're getting used to it," said Mike. "Let's go under water and find some more colourful fish."

They thoroughly enjoyed themselves in the lake until late afternoon, after which they decided to row out across the lake towards the opposite bank. Halfway across, the boys turned the boat round slightly so that everyone had a view of the craggy ridge which they knew bordered the mysterious Secret Valley.

"I reckon the pass used to be where the skyline is at its lowest," said Jack pointing. "Where the rocks are scattered higgledy-piggledy on the mountainside."

"What did you say about higs and pigs?" asked Paul, a look of amazement on his face. "Don't you mean hogs and pigs?"

"Higgledy-piggledy!" said Nora laughing. "It means all over the place with no order – like the rocks Jack's pointing to."

"Ah, I understand what you mean," said Paul. Then he gave a sigh. "You do say some funny things in English."

"We'll explore that side of the valley once we've finished with our side," said Peggy. "There are several waterfalls over there, but they don't seem to fall from the same height as the one we saw earlier. They just run down the mountainside."

"We can just see the buildings at the airbase," stated Mike, peering towards the end of the valley. "I wonder if we could row there along the river flowing out of the lake."

"Better not," said Jack at once. "We might be arrested!"

At this, Paul put on his dignified look and was about to announce he would never be arrested, then stopped, knowing that he would be teased.

"I didn't say anything, so don't look at me like that," he said grinning at the others, who were just waiting for a royal announcement.

For the next couple of days the children enjoyed themselves on the island, rowing on the lake and swimming. They had almost forgotten about the stolen plans, as there was no further reference to them. They explored the base of the mountains which frowned down upon the cabins and even found a few small caves. Pilescu kept a distant eye on Paul but allowed him almost complete freedom, much to the little prince's delight.

"How about rowing right across the lake?" suggested

Jack one morning. "We'll see if the scattered rocks do mark the old entrance to the Secret Valley."

"That sounds good," said Paul. "And we might even find a way into the valley and have another one of our adventures."

"Not this time," said Peggy shaking her head. "Pilescu said that the pass is completely blocked, so we'll certainly not have an adventure there."

But, oh dear, Peggy was wrong, quite wrong. An adventure *was* just waiting for them – and, what's more, in the Secret Valley!

The Other Side of the Valley

The children were busy packing a picnic meal to take across the lake when Pilescu, who had been on the radiophone, appeared with some very exciting news.

"Listen," he said, his fiery eyes ablaze with excitement. "Captain and Mrs Arnold will fly the new plane up and down the valley today so you will have a good view from the mountainside."

"That's great!" exclaimed Jack while everyone nodded. "We must find a fairly high spot so that we'll be able to see clearly right down the valley."

"But no climbing on the boulders," insisted Pilescu at once. "Remember what I told you about a landslide over there. Promise me you will not climb on the rocks."

"We won't do anything dangerous," promised Mike earnestly as he looked across the lake. "We'll go up the hillside a bit but we'll keep off the fallen rocks. Mind you, we'd like to see where the pass used to be."

"There was no actual road through the pass, just a track wide enough for travellers journeying through on horseback or with horse drawn carts," said Pilescu stroking his beard. "The main road around this valley has a hard surface now as the patrol Jeeps use it, but the old tracks to the pass were rough and have almost certainly disappeared. You probably won't find any."

"I bet we do!" stated Paul in a determined tone. Then a thought occurred to him. "Will the new plane land on the runway outside the cabins? We don't want to miss a close view because we're on the other side of the lake."

"Oh no," said Pilescu emphatically. "It will be flown up and down the valley to see how well it can be controlled at low speeds. It will only take off and land at the base."

"This is going to be a very enjoyable day," declared Peggy. "Especially if we do find one of the old tracks to the pass. Now, do we take one boat or both of them?"

"Just take one," answered Pilescu. "I would like to know there is another one moored in case I need it. Don't worry, I won't come spying on you. In any case, I am expecting the Jeep to bring more food and drink later this morning. Come on, I'll help you load the boat."

The tall Baronian easily carried a heavy basket in each hand as they strode down to the water's edge. He carefully stowed the baskets, checked all was well with the boat and waved goodbye as Jack took the oars and began to row strongly across the lake.

Paul started to sing a lively song in Baronian, much to the amusement of the others. On reaching the noisy chorus, he swayed from side to side, making the boat rock precariously.

"Careful, Paul!" yelled Jack struggling to regain control. "We like your lively songs, but we don't need actions to go with them and we certainly don't want to end up in the lake! What's the song about, anyway?"

"It's about freedom," replied Paul. "That's what I'm enjoying at the moment. Freedom from school and freedom from the palace."

"So are we all enjoying freedom," agreed Nora, dangling her fingers in the water. "I wonder what time Mummy and Daddy will fly down in the plane. We must keep a lookout so we don't miss them."

"What a daft thing to say!" exclaimed Mike, scornfully. "Isn't there a good chance we'll hear the plane coming?"

Everyone laughed except Nora who looked extremely crestfallen. Soon they had passed the island and were making good progress across the lake. What little breeze there was helped push them on their way. They chatted non-stop and it was not too long before they were approaching their destination.

"Now keep an eye out for a safe place to land," said Jack who, being the rower, was naturally facing away from the shore. "Somewhere we can drag the boat out of the water or where there's a bush we can tie it to."

There was, in fact, a lengthy stretch of beach although it was covered with dry earth rather than sand. Jack let the boat glide up to it, hitting the beach with a bit of a thump.

"We're here, we're here!" cried Paul excitedly, jumping over the side of the boat. He immediately let out a yell as the water was so cold.

"Mike and Peggy take a basket, while you come over here and help me with one, Paul," ordered Jack laughing at the little prince hopping about. "Nora, hold on the rope until we can drag the boat further up the beach."

"Now let's lug the baskets into the shade behind those stone walls over there," said Peggy once the boat was secure. "We don't want to leave the food in the sun."

The walls were the ruins of a farmhouse not too far

from the lake. They were merely a few feet high as the roof had long collapsed, but that was sufficient to shade the baskets from the sun.

"We'll stow them in one of the corners so they'll be in shade most of the day," decided Jack peering over the wall. "Balance them here while I jump over and lift them down."

Once the baskets were out of the way, the children had a good look at the mountainside still some way away. Two small waterfalls were tumbling down the steep face of the cliffs, resulting in two streams of sparkling water that danced down into the lake. To the left was an inviting copse of trees offering shade from the hot sun. And further along was the landslide – huge and menacing, showing off the strength of nature. It was much, much bigger than it had seemed from the cabin or the lake.

"No wonder the pass was well and truly blocked," remarked Nora looking in wonder at the jumble of rocks and boulders. "It would be almost impossible to shift all that. It all looks rather threatening. I don't think I want to bother finding the old track leading to the pass."

"Well, *we* do!" exclaimed Mike while the others nodded in agreement. "Nora, we're only going to look for an old track or path. We're not going to be stupid enough to climb on the boulders. Now let's split up and see who's going to be first to spot an old track leading to the landslide."

The children separated as they made for the hillside, although Nora tried to keep fairly close to Jack. She kept thinking the landslide might start tumbling down again. Peggy thought she had found what they were looking for, but soon realised it was the road which went right round the valley and was used by the patrol Jeeps.

Some of the boulders were perilously close to the road, although most were further up the mountain. The children's eyes were glued to the ground as they walked slowly along but there was no sign of an old path leading up the mountainside.

It was Paul who found it. He had been the last out of the ruined farmhouse and, instead of running across the grassy area, he followed a weed-covered gravelly strip going from the ruins, across the road, and towards the steep mountainside where it led away from the landslide. Then it abruptly turned back on itself. "I'm the first to find a track, it's here!" he yelled triumphantly as the others rushed over to him. "I bet this is it. It's wide enough for a horse and cart."

"You're right, this must be one of the tracks leading to the pass," agreed Jack looking carefully at the ground. "I expect there are similar ones the other side of the landslide. We didn't get that far."

"Let's follow this track and see exactly where it leads," suggested Mike setting off up the hillside. "Hey, it turns away from the landslide up here. It must lead somewhere else."

"I expect it zigzags all the way up," observed Jack. "It's the only way for a horse to climb a steep hillside. Yes, look. It turns back on itself up there."

Mike continued climbing and, sure enough, the path came into view again. It led towards the landslide then zigzagged back along the hillside.

"Perhaps this track will lead us into the Secret Valley," said Paul hopefully as he tried to keep up with Jack and Mike. "Maybe the pass wasn't completely blocked."

"No chance of that," declared Peggy, indicating the mass of boulders and rocks on their left. "I bet the path will suddenly disappear into that lot."

Peggy was right. After more zigzagging, the path disappeared into the landslide and could no longer be safely followed. Looking around, the children saw they were well up the mountain, but there was no sign of a pass into a valley on the other side. They did, however, notice that the skyline above the landslide was much lower than anywhere else. Not too far away was the little group of trees beyond which one of the waterfalls tumbled down the hillside.

"Isn't that a cave up there?" asked Nora pointing to a hollow some distance above the trees.

Looking up to where Nora was indicating, Jack nimbly leapt up the mountainside to what did indeed look like a cave. "The entrance is almost blocked by a huge boulder from the landslide," he called back. "Beyond that there does seem to be a cave. I'm going in."

"Wait for us, and be careful!" called Mike as he and the others climbed up the steep hillside. They reached the entrance just as Jack appeared from the depths of this strange cave with a boulder for a porch.

"It doesn't lead anywhere as far as I can tell," said Jack sounding disappointed. "It goes round a corner so it becomes quite dark but it looks as though the other end is blocked by a fallen boulder rather like this huge one here."

"If it led anywhere it would be common knowledge by now," pointed out Peggy. "I don't suppose you're the first person to enter the cave. Well, all this climbing has made me hot and hungry. Let's go down and have a swim."

Everyone agreed, so down the hillside they traipsed, finding it easier to follow the zigzagging path than to attempt to walk straight down. Once beside the lake, they stripped down to their swimming costumes and splashed around in the refreshing water. Discovering a delightful spot where one of the streams entered the lake they enjoyed sitting in the stream itself, feeling the cold, pure, swiftly moving water swirling round their bodies. Even Paul did not complain about the water being cold.

Eventually Mike remarked it was time they had something to eat. They dried themselves but kept their swimming costumes on, deciding to have the picnic near the ruined farmhouse so they wouldn't have to carry the baskets around.

"I do like picnics," declared Paul, piling his plate with little tomatoes, slices of ham and thick, crusty bread. "Somehow the food always seems to taste nicer out of doors."

"We had most of our meals outdoors when we were on the Secret Island," said Peggy thinking back. "But I suppose we didn't think of them as picnics."

It was while they were eating that Nora casually looked up at the mountain tops beyond the landslide. Suddenly she stiffened and pointed. "Look! Up there!"

she cried, almost choking on the crusty piece of roll in her mouth. "There's somebody up there on the top of the mountain."

Everyone stopped eating and scanned the mountain tops. Nothing moved. There was nobody to be seen.

"You must have imagined it," said Jack. "There's no one up there. It was probably a bird."

"Don't be stupid, Jack. I may say silly things sometimes but I can tell the difference between a person and a bird and there was definitely somebody up there," insisted Nora, a defiant look on her face.

"Perhaps it was someone spying on the new plane," declared Paul angrily. "Or the thief who stole the plans. We must inform Pilescu."

"If someone's up there, which is most unlikely, one of us will spot him or her while we finish eating," said Mike helping himself to another slice of ham. Then he looked up, puzzled. "Listen, what's that sound? It can't be the plane."

A throbbing sound could be heard coming from around the bend beyond the landslide. Again the children stopped eating, looking at each other in alarm as they remembered Paul's comments about spies.

"Whatever it is, it's coming *this* way," cried Nora fearfully. "Yes, here it comes round the bend – and, oh no! There are guns on it, too! Whatever shall we do?"

Who Is on the Mountain?

"Keep still," said Jack at once. "We'll bob down behind the wall as that horrible-looking thing approaches."

The vehicle did indeed look very menacing. Heavily camouflaged, it had a gun attached to each side. The children peered above the wall as it slowly approached, hoping they would not be spotted. Then, to everyone's surprise and relief, Peggy guessed what it was.

"What idiots we are, it's an armoured vehicle patrolling the valley," she said with a laugh. "It doesn't matter if we're seen."

"Well it matters to me!" insisted Paul keeping well down. "Don't tell anyone I'm here."

As it drew level with the children, the unusual vehicle stopped and an unsmiling guard called out in Baronian. The children merely shook their heads to show they did not understand.

"Just keep well away from the hillside on our left," the man called, suddenly switching to English. "It is very dangerous. We do experiments here. You should stay over by your cabin. That side of the lake is better than this."

"We're all right, we can look after ourselves," shouted Jack, not liking the guard's attitude.

The man angrily glared back. He seemed to be about

to say something else when the driver shouted at him, engaged gear and the vehicle pulled away.

"Not exactly friendly," observed Mike. "What experiments did he mean? And this side of the lake is better in the afternoon, as the sun shines into it much longer, while the cabins are in the shadow of the mountains. Did you hear what the man said in Baronian, Paul?"

"He asked how many of you there are, when he could see for himself," replied Paul, standing up. "And he asked if any of you understood Baronian. Then he spoke in English so he must have known you're the Arnold children. The driver called him Konstantin. I didn't like him."

"I didn't either," agreed Nora. "Anyway, he's gone so let's forget about him. Now, where shall we go to see the plane?"

"Why don't we go back up to those trees?" suggested Mike, gazing up the hillside. "I know it means trudging up that hill again, but we'll have a first rate view and be sheltered from this hot sun."

Everyone agreed, as it was becoming almost uncomfortably hot. They finished eating and packed the leftover food in the baskets before slowly climbing the hillside again to the welcoming copse of trees where the ground was fairly level. There they flopped down and, regaining their breath, marvelled at the view over the lake and down the valley.

"It's like the view we had from our waterfall," said Peggy peering across the valley. "I can just see it—"

Her words were interrupted by the distant sound of

powerful engines. The noise echoed around the valley as it bounced back and forth between the mountains.

"It's it, the secret plane!" yelled Paul, pointing excitedly down the valley. "It must be!"

Five pairs of eyes became glued to the end of the valley where the sound of the engines was building to a crescendo. Something slowly rose up in the air – something shining and sparkling as it reflected the sun's rays. It quickly gathered speed as it flew almost effortlessly towards the watching children. As it drew closer, they could make out the shape of a magnificent, shiny, blue and silver plane.

"Look! Look!" cried an excited Paul, jumping up and down while pointing. "It's coming so fast, it's almost here already. Just like a beautiful bird. Doesn't it look super?"

"It certainly does," agreed Jack watching the plane's progress in awe. "Funny. It made plenty of noise taking off, but I can hardly hear it now."

"It seems to be purring like a cat," said Nora. She turned to the others. "Now we must try and attract Mummy and Daddy's attention. They don't know we're over here."

"Of course, they'll expect to see us near the cabins," said Mike. "If we all wave together when the plane comes towards us they can't fail to see us. It's nearly here. What a beauty!"

The plane was approaching fast, descending slightly as it veered over to the cabins, where the children spotted Pilescu waving. It slowed down as it circled the end of the valley and approached the eagerly watching children who began to jump up and down, waving wildly. Paul, almost beside himself with excitement, kept cheering loudly, especially when two beaming faces could be seen peering through the cockpit windows and two hands waved.

"They've seen us, they've seen us!" cried Peggy, a broad grin spreading over her face. "That's Daddy at the controls – and there's Mummy next to him. And look, there are at least two other people on board."

The aircraft flew quite low as it turned to cross the lake, making straight for the waterfall. The children held their breath as, for an awful moment, it seemed as though the plane was going to crash into the mountainside but, at the last moment, it rose steeply in the air and at great speed before making a sharp turn to the left. Once again it circled the valley to where the children were standing, lost in admiration. Both Captain and Mrs Arnold gave more hearty waves as the plane purred and whistled overhead.

"Gosh, I really thought it was going to crash into the waterfall," said Mike sounding relieved. "Can't it change course quickly? Look, here it comes again."

Once more the plane approached, this time appearing to be on a collision course with the landslide. Just as it had done a few moments earlier, it made an incredibly sharp turn before heading swiftly back down the valley. However, it did not land, but flew back at a much faster speed and a higher level before finally returning to its base and landing.

"Wasn't that thrilling?" said Paul rubbing his hands in glee. "The way it turned! I'm so proud of it – and of

your parents for flying it."

"Wouldn't it be great to have a ride in the plane?" said Jack, wistfully gazing down the valley. "It must be ever so exciting seeing the mountains approaching then turning at the last minute."

"I could demand a ride," said Paul at once. "In fact, I think I will!"

"That's one thing you can't demand," said Peggy at once. "You're a Prince of Baronia so you won't be allowed to fly in a plane being tested."

"I *will* fly in it if I want to!" snapped Paul stubbornly, making the others laugh at the indignant look on his face. "Who's going to stop me? Go on. Tell me."

"I will," replied Mike solemnly. "Your father, the King."

Paul, looking defiant, wanted to argue, but instead he pursed his lips without uttering a reply, as he knew Mike was right. The King would certainly not allow one of his sons to ride in a plane undergoing trials. Paul would have to wait.

"Never mind, you're bound to fly in the plane one day," reasoned Nora not liking to see the little prince upset. "In fact, you'll probably own one."

"Well, I don't know about you, but the excitement has made me ready for another swim," said Jack looking longingly at the sparkling lake below. "Are you coming?"

Once again the five children enjoyed swimming and generally splashing around in the cooling water then they sat in one of the streams. It was when the conversation turned back to the new plane that Nora made everyone jump by letting out a yell.

"Look, there *is* someone up there!" she squealed, pointing to the mountain top beyond the landslide. "I've just seen whoever it was stand up for a moment."

The others looked at the skyline Nora was still pointing to but, again, could not make out any movement. They were convinced poor Nora's imagination was playing tricks on her when there came a sudden flash of light. This time all the children spotted it.

"Sorry, Nora, you were right," said Jack looking serious. "That flash was almost certainly caused by field glasses reflecting the sun's rays. If so, they must have been pointing at us!"

"So somebody *is* spying on the secret plane!" declared Paul. "We must definitely let Pilescu know immediately. Come. Let's get to the boat."

"Hold on just a minute," said Mike, splashing an indignant Paul. "It's probably a guard watching from the mountainside. Pilescu said there are guards on the slopes of the mountains."

"On the slopes but why on the top?" demanded Paul, his eyes blazing. "There's nothing to guard up there. Any guards would be near to where the plane is or at the entrance to this valley. It's a spy I tell you!"

"Well, I can't see any movement and there are no more flashes," said Peggy calmly. "Look how steep the mountainside is where we saw the flash. It's almost sheer, like a cliff. Nobody could climb up there. Perhaps something else caused the flash."

"I saw somebody," insisted Nora. "I agree with Paul that we should inform Pilescu."

"We'll certainly do that when we return," said Jack. "Now that the plane has been and gone there's nothing for your spy to spy on."

"Yes there is," replied Paul at once. "There's the airbase. It can be clearly seen from up there. The spy may be the one who stole the plans or have you forgotten about them? And he probably lives in the Secret Valley. He may even come from Maldonia."

"You can see for yourself that nobody can get into or out of the Secret Valley," said Mike with a grin. "Now listen, I've an idea. If there really is someone keeping watch on the base and the plane, then he'll be there each day. Why don't we ask Pilescu if we can camp under those trees for a couple of nights? We can have a bit of fun over here and see if our spy appears again – although I still think it's a guard."

"Yes, that *is* a good idea, we will do that!" agreed Paul, his eyes lighting up. "It will be so nice to sleep under the stars – and even better if we catch a spy."

Everyone laughed. "You and your spies!" exclaimed Peggy. "If it's a spy, we're not likely to catch him. Anyway, we can't possibly climb the mountain as it's too steep. It's bad enough climbing the hillside."

"We'll ask Pilescu as soon as we return to the cabin," said Jack. "Now let's enjoy ourselves in the lake before we go back."

As soon as they returned to their cabin at the end of the day they consulted Pilescu about Mike's idea of spending a couple of nights on the other side of the valley.

"I have to fly to the palace tomorrow," he replied.

"And, as your parents have a very important meeting, they cannot come down here so I don't see why you should not camp on the hillside. After all, you looked after yourselves for months on your island. Now, if I remember correctly, there are a couple of tents in a shed behind the cabin. These will offer you some shelter at night. Come and see for yourselves."

Five very excited children found the two tents which would accommodate them, plenty of pegs, and an oil stove on which they could do some cooking. They were so engrossed in sorting everything out that they did not remember to tell Pilescu about the person they thought they saw on the mountain until they were having their evening meal.

"If it was a person, then it was almost certainly Konstantin or Mikaelo who keep watch from the mountainside," said Pilescu with a frown. "I know Mikaelo's on duty now, as he has taken over from Konstantin who was in the Jeep. Nobody can approach the buildings or planes without being challenged, but I will certainly report what you have told me."

"Well, if it is a spy, we'll catch him," declared Paul, making everyone laugh. "Even if we have to chase him into the Secret Valley. Hurry up, tomorrow!"

The next morning, the children were up early and, after a hearty breakfast, hurried down to the lake with food and blankets. Pilescu had already tied the tents securely to the side of the boat and made certain that the pegs and a hammer were on board, as well as torches with spare batteries.

They were about to cast off when they became

aware of a low flying plane. There it was, darting back and forth across the valley as though searching for something. Then a Jeep appeared and pulled up near the lake. A uniformed guard hurriedly jumped out and spoke earnestly to Pilescu. After a short conversation in low voices, Pilescu turned to address the children, a serious look on his face.

"Another awful thing has happened," he said solemnly. "Kyril informed me that a piece of the secret plane's engine was removed during the night. It's small, but vital and still secret. Fortunately we have a spare, but that's not the point. Someone has stolen one of our inventions. There is an enemy in the valley."

"Or… on the mountain," added Nora, gazing across the lake.

A Terrifying Storm

The shocked children could scarcely believe their ears. How could anybody steal an important part of the plane when everything would be so well guarded – especially bearing in mind what had already occurred?

"Tell the guard about the person on the mountain," urged Nora. "I bet he had something to do with all this."

Pilescu informed the guard who, to the children's surprise, simply gave a wry smile.

"Kyril says Konstantin and Mikaelo were keeping watch on the mountainside yesterday, so you probably saw one of them," said Pilescu translating. "Two small planes are out searching, one we can see flying over the mountain tops, another following the River Jollu."

"Well, we'll certainly keep a look out from our camp," promised Jack. "If we notice anything suspicious, we'll wave something large like a shirt at the next plane or Jeep we see."

"I will row across to see you when I return tomorrow, my little lord," said Pilescu to Paul. "Just to check all is well. But now I must accompany Kyril to the base for the latest news as I shall have to report the details of this unpleasantness to the King later today."

Saying goodbye, the children clambered aboard the heavily laden boat. The extra weight made progress across the lake quite slow even though both Jack and Mike were rowing. Nora kept her eyes glued to the skyline but saw nobody. Having heard about the guards watching from the mountainside, the others did not bother to look in that direction. They were too busy chatting about their camping adventure.

As soon as they reached the shore, they tied the boat to a shrub before removing various items and placing them on the grass. After that, they untied the tents, storing the rope in the box with the tent pegs, as they would need it on the return journey.

"Mike and I will take a tent each. The girls can bring the food, while, Paul, you carry the box of pegs and torches," instructed Jack. "We'll collect the other things when we come down for a swim."

The little party crossed the grassy plain before slowly ascending the steep hill to the copse of trees. Once there, they put their goods on the ground and sat down to regain their breath as the air was becoming unusually humid.

"It's such a toil up this hill!" exclaimed Peggy, still puffing. "Especially when carrying things."

"As soon as we get our breath back, we'll find places for the tents," decided Mike, looking around. "It's fairly level under these trees as long as we avoid their roots."

The thought of putting up the tents gave everyone renewed energy, but it was not as easy as they had expected. In fact, both tents kept falling down until Jack organised the erecting of one tent at a time. Eventually, both were in position, sheltered by the trees. The ground was somewhat uneven, so the children were glad there were tough blankets still in the boat.

Nora suggested they should collect tufts of heather to put under the blankets. "It will be like having a springy mattress," she said. Then she added, "Just like on our island on Lake Wildwater."

Nearby was one of the ever-tumbling waterfalls, so there would be no shortage of fresh water. They agreed to use the lower part for washing themselves and for doing the washing up and the upper section for clean, clear drinking water. In the other direction was the landslide, while above them towered the mountains, seeming to almost touch the blue sky.

The children had great fun in the waterfall. It wasn't really a big fall but a series of little ones that cascaded down the mountainside to the lake. In one place the water fell into a large, hollowed out boulder, rather like a rock pool on a beach. They were able to safely sit at the edge of this pool enjoying the soft, cold and frothy water, just right for a hot, humid day.

While enjoying themselves in the pool, they heard the sound of an engine and saw Pilescu take off in Paul's plane. The children waved as he circled above them before disappearing over the mountains.

It was towards evening as they were sorting out some food, when Peggy became intrigued by strange coloured clouds building up over the mountains on the other side of the valley. The clouds were dark but with weird purple and orange hues.

"I don't like the look of those clouds," she said pointing across the valley. "That looks like rain on the way."

"That's more than rain, it's a storm building up,"

said Jack looking intensely at the darkening sky. "Luckily those clouds are on the far side of the mountains and following the tops. Hopefully the storm will miss us altogether although, I must say, it has felt humid all day."

"As long as the storm is over there it won't interfere with our meal," stated Mike, carefully placing the oil stove on some level ground. "We'll fry some sausages and eggs and heat up some beans to go with them. Playing around in the waterfall and swimming in the lake has given me quite an appetite."

Indeed, all five had built up considerable appetites and did full justice to the meal. There was juicy fresh fruit for dessert which was greatly appreciated. Naturally, Paul had insisted on Pilescu packing plenty of creamy Baronian chocolate to eat during the evening, although it had become rather soft and gooey in the heat.

As soon as darkness fell, the children chatted beside the waterfall, then had lemonade and biscuits before retreating into their tents, planning to get up early in the morning. They had wanted to have a camp fire but Jack sensibly realised it would be too dangerous. "A fire would easily spread out of control in these dry conditions," he said to the others, "and there would be no way of putting it out. Never mind, we can have one down by the lake tomorrow night."

For a while they talked in their tents then, tired out, they dropped off to sleep one by one. During the night, Nora was awakened by a strange plopping sound against the canvas. Feeling scared, she woke a disgruntled Peggy who fumbled for her torch. Cautiously peering outside, she saw the cause of the weird sound.

"Drat! It's raining," she said, hastily retreating back into the tent and shining the torch on the canvas. "The plops are drops of water falling off the trees. At least the tent seems to be waterproof. Just go back to sleep."

They were just dropping off to sleep when an even stranger sound awoke them. It was like a gigantic drum roll echoing around the valley. Now it was Peggy's turn to sit up.

"Whatever was that?" she asked as the sound faded away. "What's happening?"

As if to answer her question, a vivid flash could be seen somewhere down the valley, followed by more rumblings, this time louder and seemingly closer.

"Oh no, it's a storm!" exclaimed Nora in dismay. "It's coming our way. I don't like storms. Let's wake the boys."

They dashed over to the boys' tent, almost tripping over a couple of the tent pegs. The boys were already awake, having been disturbed by the rumbling thunder.

"There's no room in here so go back to your own tent," moaned Mike putting his torch down. "I've just checked the canvas so it's quite waterproof. We should remain dry."

"Don't be too sure of that," said Jack sleepily. "The ground is fairly level under the trees but it doesn't alter the fact that we're on a hillside. If there is enough water to run down from the mountain, we're going to get rather wet."

Then all five jumped as a bright flash seemed to dance around the valley. A short while afterwards there followed a loud clap of thunder which resounded ominously around the mountainsides.

"I don't like us being here in a storm," said Nora, fighting back her tears as she crouched down. "It's very scary. What shall we do?"

"One thing is for certain," stated Jack, now wide awake. "If that storm gets any closer we can't remain under trees. There are only about five of them, so there is a real risk of one being struck by lightning. And that would be very, very dangerous for us."

"Wherever can we go?" asked Mike in alarm. "We can't return across the lake in the dark and we can't wander about on the mountainside as any one of us could be struck by lightning."

Suddenly everyone held their breath as there was another brilliant flash of lightning, the thunder following in a matter of seconds. "It's no use, we must move away from these trees at all costs as the storm is coming closer by the second," stated Jack in a determined voice. "We'd better make for the ruins by the lake, not that there's much in the way of shelter – and the wind's strengthening."

"Why don't we go up to the cave we saw yesterday?" suggested Paul. "It's just above us, so it is closer than the ruins. We would be safe in there."

"Of course – good idea, Paul," agreed Mike. "Let's do that, Jack. We'll be dry as well as safe."

"Yes, that's a super idea," said a relieved Jack. "At least we'll be away from the lightning – that is what worries me. Put shoes on and bring clothes, torches, the pack of spare batteries, towels and the food, so it won't be ruined if water runs down the hillside."

"And we'd better bring our blankets," added Peggy making for her tent. "The floor of the cave is bound to be rough."

"I'll lead the way while you bring up the rear, Mike," ordered Jack, flashing his torch on the ground. "Use your torch as well, Nora."

It was not easy finding their way up the uneven hillside through the buffeting wind and stinging rain with only limited torchlight to guide them, as the dark clouds completely blocked out any moonlight. Every now and again lightning flashed – forked lightning! They stumbled and tripped up the hillside until they had reached the cave, where water was dripping from the boulder over the entrance.

Jack put the food basket on the floor then hurried back down to fetch the blankets from the boys' tent,

realising that they would have to spend the night in the cave. Another flash of lightning lit him up, making the boy look like a ghost scrambling back up the hillside. This was followed by an extremely loud roll of thunder, very heavy rain and a howling wind.

"Thank goodness you thought of the cave, Paul," said Jack throwing the blankets on the floor and patting the prince on the back. "Otherwise I don't know what we'd have done, as there's no shelter anywhere. We'd be absolutely drenched. I'm wet through as it is. Where's my towel?"

More flashes, sometimes two at a time, lit up the valley and the lake, followed almost immediately by claps of thunder which seemed to make the hillside tremble. The rain, which had been steadily falling, now became torrential, pouring off the overhanging boulder and running down the hill in all directions like little waterfalls.

"The storm's overhead," said Peggy fearfully. "There's hardly a gap between the lightning and the thunder. I don't like it one bit."

"Don't worry, we're safe in here," said Mike sounding more confident than he felt.

Then everyone jumped. An incredibly bright stream of light seemed to hit one of the trees down below. There was loud hiss followed by a sheet of flame that was quickly extinguished by the heavy rain. Almost immediately came a clap of thunder which caused the huge stone at the entrance to the cave to shudder as though it was about to collapse.

"Keep back," ordered Jack, his mouth and throat

suddenly feeling dry. "One of the trees has been struck and now this stone here doesn't look very safe."

"There's going to be another landslide," wailed Nora now in tears. "And this cave is going to collapse. We'll be swept down the mountain!"

Jack shone his torch on the walls of the cave. "It's all right, Nora. These walls won't collapse. They're solid rock. It's that stone I'm worried about. Oh no, more lightning!"

This time the streaks of lightning were not only accompanied by deafening thunder claps but by a tremendous roar on the hillside itself. The cave shook as pieces of rock and stone tumbled down across the entrance. The overhanging boulder dropped again, dislodging small pieces of rock. Then came an extra loud roar as though the mountain itself were collapsing. The boulder gave way and terrifyingly crashed down. Tons of debris from the mountain fell on top of it, filling every nook and cranny.

By the eerie light of a torch, five horrified children gaped at the awful sight. Their exit from the cave was now well and truly blocked! They were trapped!

The Passage through the Mountain

For a moment nobody uttered a word. Jack put his arm round Nora, who was quietly sobbing. The sound of the storm had become more distant, muffled by the fallen boulder and its covering of smaller rocks and stones. Everywhere there was the smell of dust.

"Whatever are we going to do?" asked Peggy, after a while. "We're trapped, trapped inside a mountain and nobody knows we're here. However will we get out? Do something, Jack!"

"I don't think it would be wise to do anything while it's night time and there's a terrible storm raging out there," answered Jack, desperately trying to come up with a better, more positive response. "We're dry and, more importantly, safe from the lightning. If we had been in our tents when the lightning struck that tree, we might all have been killed."

There was further silence as the children thought of the tragedy that could so easily have befallen them. As Jack said, they were safe – for the time being.

"A ghastly thought has just occurred to me," said Mike shining his torch on the rubble. "This entrance looks completely blocked. Are we likely to run out of air?"

"There may be gaps in the fallen rocks," said Jack, peering at the debris. "It's hard to tell, as it's dark outside. I'll tell you what I'll do. I'll go further back into the cave where the fallen rock is that I saw yesterday. There might be air coming in there, as the stone had to fall from somewhere. Just keep one torch on while I'm away. I know we have spare batteries, but we don't want to waste them."

He cautiously made his way towards the back of the cave. Going round a corner, his torch lit up the rock he had seen before. However, to his surprise and alarm, there was a fresh pile of rubble in front of it. Above and around it there seemed to be gaps which he could not recall noticing on his previous visit. However, the most important thing was a definite current of fresh air passing through the gaps. Feeling the draught, Jack hurriedly returned to the others.

"The rock at the back of the cave has shifted downwards since yesterday, although there's plenty of fresh air passing through from somewhere," he explained sounding relieved. "I really believe that the most sensible thing to do now is to try to get some sleep, as we can do nothing while it's night time. Good job we brought the blankets and jerseys, even if they are a bit wet."

"The beds won't be very comfortable," moaned Nora. "There's just a hard stone floor. It'll be awful."

"Well, I'm so tired I could sleep anywhere," said Paul giving a loud yawn. "Why don't we spread our blankets over here, Jack? The floor's almost level and there are plenty of soft, grassy bits."

"The grassy bits are called moss so they'll be a bit springy for a while," said Mike with a grin. "Fancy having to lie on the floor of a cave again. I'll never manage to get to sleep."

But he did, and so did the others. They had had plenty of exercise during the day and being awakened from their sleep by the storm caused them to be extremely tired by the time they finally settled on the makeshift beds.

As they slept, the storm disappeared over the mountains and the rain gradually ceased. The children were still fast asleep when dawn broke and sunshine again began to fill the valley, not that they could see anything from the darkness of their cave. Mike woke up first, feeling extremely stiff. Rubbing his neck, he fumbled for his torch and shone it on his watch. It was eight o'clock.

"Gosh! Jack, wake up!" he said urgently, giving Jack a prod. "It's eight o'clock already and we've got to try to escape from this horrible cave."

At first, Jack merely grunted, then, as it dawned on him where they were, he sat up, rubbing his back. "I ache all over," he grumbled, pulling a face. "The floor seemed to get harder and harder during the night. Better wake the others and we'll have something to eat before deciding what to do."

Rubbing various aches, the five children ate a hurried breakfast by torchlight, glad they had thought of bringing the food into the cave. The meal over, they now had to decide exactly what to do to try to find some way of escaping. Nora secretly feared they would be stuck inside for ever, although refrained from saying so.

First, they inspected the boulder and rubble at the entrance. There was no gap anywhere. No daylight could be seen. It was impossible to tell how many rocks and stones were piled up behind the boulder.

"Can't we push some of the stones out of the way?" suggested Paul, beginning to feel afraid. "If we make a hole we could shout through it and be rescued."

"Whatever we do, we mustn't risk a further landslide in front of the cave or we'll never be found," replied Jack solemnly. "Don't forget, we could be badly injured if rocks actually fell on us. No, first let's have a good look at the other end of the cave. That fresh air has to come from somewhere."

He led everyone round the corner where the huge rock was blocking the way. Shining the torches through the gaps at the side of this stone, they were surprised to discover that the cave seemed to become a tunnel leading round another corner out of sight.

Jack shone his torch at the roof above the fallen rock. "I do believe we could scramble through the largest of the gaps as long as we're careful not to dislodge any more stones," he said. "The piles of rubble were caused by last night's storm, so there could be more stones waiting to fall. We must see where the tunnel leads."

"The trouble is, if we go this way we are going further into the mountain," pointed out Peggy. "We need to escape from it, not go further in."

"We've been around one corner and we can see there's another ahead, so the passage might double back on itself and come out somewhere else on the mountainside," suggested Mike. "It must lead somewhere outside because of all the fresh air."

"Well, if it does, I hope it doesn't come out on

the landslide," said Nora. "Then we really would be trapped."

"No we wouldn't because we could signal for help," said Paul. "Pilescu knows we're over here, so he will arrange a search party."

"Don't forget Mikaelo and Konstantin are somewhere on the mountain," added Mike. "It will be good if this passage leads to the landslide. Let's move, Jack."

"We'll squeeze through this large gap here one at a time," decided Jack. "If anything seems to about to fall, get out of the way immediately. I'll go first. Shine my torch on me, Peggy."

The others anxiously watched as Jack climbed up to where there was a gap between the wall of the cave and the fallen rock. Carefully checking the roof to make sure no further falls were likely, he eased his body through the gap and lowered himself down on to the pile of rubble on the other side. Heaving a sigh of relief, he stood up and poked his head through the gap.

"Go and fetch our belongings," he said. "We may well need them on this side."

The others kept tripping over the blankets as they hurriedly fetched everything. One by one, the items were passed through to Jack who then called through the gap. "If you hand me my torch, Peggy, I'll shine it on the gap while you, Nora and Paul pass through with your torches. Mike, you bring up the rear."

Paul and the girls heaved themselves through, each growing alarmed as small stones dropped on to them from the roof. Finally it was Mike's turn. He was almost through the gap when, unfortunately, his foot seemed to become stuck against an awkwardly shaped stone. In a panic, he tugged as hard as he could with his leg and dislodged the stone which, in turn, caused a large amount of debris to come noisily crashing down. Then a huge rock fell, completely blocking the way. Miraculously, Mike was not hurt, but he did fall to the ground with quite a bump.

"Gosh, I don't like the look of that," said Jack shining his torch on the fallen rocks. "We'll never be able to return this way. It'll be impossible to move those rocks and stones. What about you? Are you all right, Mike?"

"I think so," replied Mike, hopping about. "My leg hurts a bit. I thought I was stuck and had visions of the roof caving in on me. I'll be all right so let's press on, Captain, and see where the cave leads."

"It's more like a passage now," observed Peggy noticing the walls becoming closer. "I wonder what's around the bend."

The roof became much lower and the floor of the tunnel became very uneven. The children had to tread carefully to avoid twisting an ankle or hitting their heads on the many low bulges in the roof. Progress was quite slow. Ahead was yet another bend, past which the floor had puddles on it from drops of water falling down from the damp roof. Gleaming in the torchlight, the walls were also damp, with moss growing here and there on the rock.

"I wonder if this dampness means we're near the waterfall," said Nora.

"I shouldn't think so or we'd hear it," replied Peggy. "It's very quiet in this passage. The water must be

something to do with all that rain last night. Look, there's another bend ahead. I seem to have lost track of which direction we're going in."

"Well, *I* think we're going further into the mountain," said Mike, to everyone's dismay. "The twists and turns have been in different directions. They would all need to be in the same direction if we're to come out by one of the waterfalls or the landslide."

This was alarming news. It would be awful to end up in the middle of the mountain, especially as the passage was blocked behind them. On and on they stumbled until, to their great delight, they went round a bend and saw a faint light shining on the rocky wall ahead.

"That must be daylight so, hopefully, a way out at last!" exclaimed Jack, a smile now spreading across his face for the first time that morning. "Come on! Let's get

round the next corner."

Almost forgetting the bumpy floor and the uneven roof, they traipsed along to where the passage narrowed considerably, turned abruptly and then opened out to become more like a cave again. A fairly smooth platform surrounded by rocks protruded from the cave.

Jack at once went out onto this platform, expecting to find a view of the lake and their valley. "That's funny," he said, turning to the others, a puzzled look on his face. "I thought there'd be a steep drop, but there are more rocks and boulders obscuring the view. And there's the landslide to our left. Thank goodness that storm has completely disappeared."

The others joined Jack. Seeing only rocks in front of them and mountains in the background, they looked for a way off the platform. Jack squeezed between two upright rocks, finding what resembled a path just below, leading from the landslide. Above was the almost sheer face of the mountain. The children moved a short way along the path to a spot where there were no rocks, just the bare, sloping mountainside. All five gasped in awe.

They were gazing down into a strange and wild valley surrounded by mountains with sheer faces. Nearby they could see and hear a waterfall tumbling down to a small lake. The floor of the valley was littered with rocks, boulders and stones except for a small grassy area near the lake. There was all manner of vegetation including wild flowers although, surprisingly, there were few trees. Scattered around the valley were sad, derelict cottages, many without roofs, almost certainly old farmhouses. There were no sheep, no horses, no cattle. The only signs of life were the colourful birds flying around, taking no notice of their new visitors.

Over the mountains the sun was shining, the only reminder of the storm being little puddles among the rocks. A gentle breeze was blowing causing the air to feel pleasantly fresh. Reflected in the lake down below were the cloudless blue sky and the far mountains.

"Gosh, where on earth *are* we?" asked Jack looking around in wonder. "It's a beautiful valley, but it's not ours. It's too small. I think I must be dreaming."

Nobody answered as they gazed, spellbound, at the surprising view. Suddenly Paul broke the silence. "*I* know where we are!" he cried, rubbing his hands excitedly. "We're in the valley on the other side of our mountains. You know – the one where nobody lives. We have found a way into the Secret Valley!"

In the Secret Valley

The children continued to stare open-mouthed, first at the remarkable view, then at each other.

"I do believe you're right, Paul," declared an astonished Mike. "We're in the Secret Valley, the first people to be here since the enormous landslide. That's super!"

"No, it isn't," pointed out an anxious Nora, looking earnestly at the others. "Just think. Nobody lives in the Secret Valley. Nobody enters the Secret Valley. Nobody will suspect we're in the Secret Valley. So, how do we leave?"

"Nora's got a point, as we can't possibly climb up the mountainside," said Peggy, turning to look at the steep, rugged cliffs all around. "The entrance to our tunnel is completely blocked and possibly hidden. The only place the ridge drops is blocked by a landslide we daren't climb over. The rubble could give way any moment."

"That's obviously where the track over the mountain used to be," said Mike. He turned to gaze at the far end of the valley. "Look, the skyline dips down there as well. That's where the third landslide happened. You can see all the boulders."

"There'll be a search party looking for us as soon as they realise we're missing and someone may know there's a cave behind the fallen rocks," observed Jack confidently. "Search planes are bound to fly overhead so we must be ready to wave. We need to be where we can be seen, so let's go down to that lake." He looked around. "I reckon we could make our way down between those low rocks over there."

There was indeed something which resembled an overgrown path, twisting and turning between stones and boulders, all the time leading downwards. Much of the vegetation was taller than the children, offering welcome shelter from the heat of the morning sun but hiding them from any search plane that might fly over them. Sweet purple bilberries grew in many places on the mountainside and there were even wild raspberries.

Having eventually reached the valley floor, they perched on rocks near the calm lake. Behind them towered the mountains, while nearby was a sparkling stream which had danced merrily down the hillside in a series of waterfalls. The lake was quite small, the Secret Valley itself being much smaller than the one in which they were staying.

"You can almost imagine Beowald appearing from behind a rock," remarked Peggy, recalling their previous holiday in Baronia. "At least he would know a way out of the valley."

The children were still chatting about their predicament when, to their amazement, something small leapt up to them, turned, and hopped back towards the water. And then the same thing happened again – and again.

"Toads!" exclaimed Jack in delight. "They're usually

shy creatures, but these don't seem to be in the least bit afraid of us. Look at the strange orange marks on their backs."

"They're just like the ones we have near our lake at the palace," observed Paul. He started giggling. "My mother always runs away from them."

While they were watching the energetic antics of the toads, Mike sharply drew in his breath, making everyone look at him in amazement. With a trembling hand, he pointed to the ground a short distance away. The others looked and gasped. There was something they had not expected to see in the deserted Secret Valley – footprints!

"They're not ours, as we haven't been over there," said Mike, taking a closer look.

"This is really weird, and possibly serious," said Jack joining him. "There are clearly two different prints here. I think we'd better not stay in the open like this, as the prints almost certainly belong to the enemy."

"The enemy!" exclaimed Nora, looking all around in alarm. "What enemy?"

"Have you forgotten that the plans and an engine part were stolen?" reminded Jack. "What better place to hide with them than in the Secret Valley? Or worse." With a serious expression, he looked towards the far end of the valley. "They could be taken to Maldonia!"

"Do you really think whoever stole the plans is here?" asked a surprised Mike. "How could he have got into the Secret Valley?"

"That would be the first question we'd be asked if someone came across us," replied Jack. "The fact is, two sets of prints are there, so we need to find out who made them and where they are now. The footprints are fresh or they would have been washed away in last night's heavy rain. At least two people are in this valley apart from ourselves, maybe more. And they might be watching us at this *very* moment."

This was not a pleasant thought. There was a moment's silence as everyone gazed around fearfully, imagining hidden eyes were peering at them from behind every bush and around every rock.

"We're having one of our adventures, aren't we?" said Peggy, breaking the silence. "Our second in Baronia. Well, if we haven't already been spotted, we will be, wandering in a big group. Perhaps we ought to split up. And mind we don't leave footprints!"

"Let's go and keep watch from that platform," begged Paul, not liking the idea that enemies of his country might be nearby. "It seemed safe there."

"That's a good idea," agreed Nora. "We can easily see the whole valley."

"I know it sounds a good idea, but the problem is that, if we're on the platform, we won't be able to make ourselves seen if a plane flies overhead," observed Mike. "Part of the cliff face is overhanging. Besides, we don't want to spend all day up there, do we?"

"So why not take it in turns to be lookouts while the others do a bit of exploring nearby?" suggested Peggy. "I'll take first watch for an hour or so."

"That sounds sensible, Peggy, but it really needs two to keep watch properly," said Jack. "If a stranger is spotted, one of those watching can keep an eye on whoever it is while the other hurries to warn the rest of us. Agreed?"

Everyone agreed this was the most sensible thing to do. So Mike went with Peggy to take the first watch while Jack led Nora and Paul up alongside the little waterfall. They were delighted to find a small pool like the one on the other side of the mountain where they could sit and dangle their legs in the cool tumbling water, hidden from view by surrounding rocks.

Mike and Peggy found places on the platform where, between them, they could see most of the valley, although the tall vegetation and the many boulders would hide anyone from view much of the time.

"At least we should be able to detect any movement in the valley," said Mike confidently. "After all, whoever is in this valley won't expect anyone to be watching for them, so they won't be deliberately hiding or be particularly careful."

"They must have somewhere to stay and keep their food," pointed out Peggy. "Look for some sort of building. The ruins we can see are hardly habitable."

"I'll concentrate on the right-hand side of the valley and you watch the left-hand side," said Mike. "We might spot something interesting. I'll keep an eye on that derelict farmhouse over there."

Although Mike kept noticing movements in the valley, they were always caused by large birds. He had a good view of the entire mountainside as it was so bare, not that he expected to see anybody on it. Satisfied there was nobody by the lake or waterfalls, he concentrated on the far side of the valley but there was no sign of human life.

Peggy also had a good view of the bare mountains, but fixed her gaze on the land around the left-hand side of the lake, wishing she was enjoying herself by the waterfall with the other three. Gradually, after her uncomfortable night, she yawned and began to feel drowsy in the heat. Her imagination seemed to be running away with her when she thought she saw a man appear from nowhere, standing near the lake.

"Now I'm dreaming while I'm supposed to be keeping watch," she muttered angrily, shaking her head to wake herself up. "This will never do."

Filling her lungs with deep breaths and pinching herself, she felt wide awake again and looked over to where she thought she had seen the man, smiling at

the very thought of it. Her smile quickly vanished. He wasn't a dream – he was *real*. He was still there!

"Mike," she called urgently. "There's someone to the left of the lake. Look! I was feeling tired so thought I was dreaming. I wasn't. He's real enough. See?"

Mike moved over to where his sister was watching and opened his mouth in amazement. "Gosh! Where did he come from? Did you notice?"

"No," replied Peggy, keeping her eyes on the man. "He simply appeared while I was looking at the ruined cottage down there, although I didn't notice him come from it."

"Right, we must inform the others in case they're spotted by him," said Mike. "Keep watching while I go to the waterfall."

Before Peggy could reply, Mike quickly disappeared between the rocks and boulders as he carefully made his way down to the waterfall, guided by the sound of the falling water and by the occasional raised voice. Soon he was beside the cascading fall and saw Jack, Nora and Paul a short distance below, sitting on rocks enjoying the frothy water dancing merrily around their bare feet.

"Jack," shouted Mike, knowing the sound of the water would drown his voice. All three turned at once. "There's a man about halfway down the left side of the lake. Mind he doesn't see you."

Paul and Nora at once wanted to peer round the rocks at the man, but Jack hastily pulled them back. "You'll be in full view," he reminded them as he reached for his shoes. "What's more, we know there's more than one person around because of the footprints. You two go back with Mike. I'm going to try to discover where his hiding place is. It must be down there somewhere or he wouldn't risk standing in the open in case a plane comes over."

"Take care, Jack," called Mike as Jack stealthily crept down the mountainside, all the while keeping behind rocks and tall vegetation. Every so often, he risked peering over a boulder to check that he was going in the right direction and that the man wasn't coming his way.

From her position near the entrance to the passage, Peggy was alarmed to see Jack actually making his way towards the figure still standing by the lake. She fervently hoped there was nobody on the mountainside, as Jack would easily be spotted from above. Then she jumped as Mike, Nora and Paul appeared. "You scared me creeping up like that," she laughed. "Come over here and watch Jack's progress. The man's still there, Mike."

"I wonder if that's the person who has stolen the plans of my country's new plane," said Paul, his fiery eyes fixed on the man by the lake. "I should have gone with Jack. I could have demanded the return of the plans."

"And I suppose he would have meekly handed them over," said Nora scornfully. "For a start, we don't know he is the thief and, if he is, we can't approach him and simply ask for the plans to be returned. Jack hopes to discover where his hiding place is so that we can tell whoever finds us."

This time it was Paul who was scornful. "So we're just going to be found, are we?" he replied. "Who is just going to find us? Who even knows we're here?"

"Stop bickering, you two," said Mike. "Look, there's Jack. He has almost reached the man."

Jack was pushing his way through the fairly thick undergrowth, then stopped in amazement. He had reached a wide, flat track. In places it was covered with grass and, apart from slight twists and turns, it was almost straight as it led to the far end of the Secret Valley.

"Of course, it's the old road linking the two passes!" the boy exclaimed to himself. "Now how do I cross it without being seen?"

The man was not far away on the other side of the track studying pieces of paper. "Could *they* be the stolen plans?" wondered Jack angrily, looking all around in case there was a second person nearby. Seeing nobody, he sprinted quietly across the track to hide behind a tall rock.

The man suddenly folded the papers, placing them

carefully into a packet, and strode into the ruins that Peggy had noticed. It was fortunate that Jack remained where he was, as the man soon reappeared, but without the packet. Then Jack's heart seemed to beat loudly and he held his breath. The stranger was approaching his hiding place.

Dreading that he may have been spotted, he prepared to dart into the dense undergrowth. Peering through the bracken, he could just make out the man's features as he came closer. Jack stared open-mouthed. No wonder, as he had seen the man before. It was the surly guard, Konstantin, who had warned the children to keep away from the mountains only two days before, and, here he was, now heading straight for him!

An Exciting Morning – and a
Bitter Disappointment

Shaking his head in disbelief, Jack crouched lower, still ready to run. However, Konstantin strode past him and went along the track towards the mountain. As soon as he felt it was safe to search the ruins, the boy darted to the old cottage, cautiously peering through what was left of the doorway in case another person was inside. There were no windows, but the walls were quite high and the roof fairly intact. Satisfied that no one was about, Jack entered.

The first room was bare, with moss on most of the walls, while the floor had weeds in the cracks between the flagstones. He entered another room, dominated by an old fireplace. At once he felt certain this was where Konstantin had hidden the packet, but the chimney had collapsed, blocking any nooks and crannies that might have been there.

There were two more rooms, although at first sight there was nothing in either to indicate where the man had been. One was the former kitchen or scullery, as it had a large old sink in one corner. The other was quite bare.

"That man Konstantin entered with a packet and definitely left without it – and it was too big for his pocket – so *where* can it be?" Jack asked himself. "I *must* search again."

Once more he searched, trying to find spaces between stones in the walls. But the walls were solid; there were no gaps. As he hung his head in despair, his attention was suddenly attracted by a flagstone around which the soil had been disturbed and no weeds were growing. What's more, an iron ring was set in the nearest end of the stone. His heart pounding, he tugged at the ring but, although the stone moved slightly, he could not raise it. He tried again and again. No, the stone refused to lift.

"There must be a way of opening it," Jack reasoned. "You can't lock a stone! Wait... I wonder if I could be pulling the wrong way..."

He positioned himself at the other end of the stone, lent forwards and tugged with all his might. This time the stone rose up so quickly that poor Jack sprawled backwards. He quickly got back on his feet. The stone had stayed upright, revealing a dark, gaping hole.

"So that's the hideout!" he exclaimed peering into the void where he could make out wooden steps leading to a room below. Listening for sounds, Jack slowly went down the steps but, at the bottom, he could not see anything in the darkness.

"If only I had my torch," he thought as he climbed back up. "I can't do any more now but I shall definitely return with a torch. This is a most important discovery."

Lowering the flagstone, he was about to leave the ruin when he stopped, sharply drawing in his breath. He had heard voices! That meant at least two people were just outside the cottage! In a panic, Jack looked for somewhere to hide, but there was absolutely nowhere. Remembering the fireplace in the next room, he dashed in there and huddled in the hearth, knowing he would be spotted at once by anybody looking around the room. No sooner was he in position than a thin, wiry man with a light brown beard appeared, followed by a tall, severe-looking dark-haired woman.

Jack held his breath as they passed through to the kitchen without glancing in his direction. There came the sound of the flagstone being raised and someone going down the wooden steps. The boy cautiously peered around the fireplace and, through the doorway, saw the upright flagstone. This was his chance to return to the others.

He eased himself out of the fireplace, but in doing so knocked his shoulder against a loose stone which fell with a resounding crash onto the floor. Naturally, the people down below heard this and stopped speaking for a moment before shouting out in a language Jack did not understand. It did not sound like Baronian.

Dashing out of the cottage, he swiftly crossed the track and dived headlong into some dense undergrowth. Almost immediately, he heard two voices calling out and dreaded that he had been spotted. Parting the drooping fronds of a thick shrub, he peered in the direction of the ruin.

The two people were looking around some rocks near the cottage, obviously unconvinced that the stone had fallen by accident. The man began to peer up and down the valley while the woman turned away from the cottage and, to Jack's horror, crossed the track, coming in his direction.

He bobbed down, hearing her push vegetation aside as she approached. Huge boulders prevented him from wriggling to either side and, if he moved forwards, he would be seen instantly. On she came. Poor Jack felt extremely alarmed. She was now just two or three steps away and about to tread on him. He would have to run or be caught!

Then an amazing thing happened. The woman stopped in her tracks, gave a loud scream, and retreated. Immediately Jack tried to see what had scared her. Once again his heart almost missed a beat as something jumped off the boulder down beside him and leapt back up. Jack just managed to stifle a laugh. It was only a toad!

Hearing the man roar with laughter and the woman angrily shouting at him, Jack peeped above the boulders and saw the two return to the cottage. As soon as he was satisfied they did not pose further danger, he returned as quickly as possible to the mountainside, dodging around rocks, boulders and shrubs.

"Thank goodness for the waterfall and landslide," he thought as he stumbled along. "They're perfect landmarks. At least I know the platform is between them. I wonder if the others saw the man and woman follow me into the cottage."

The other children had, indeed, seen part of the happenings and experienced some excitement themselves. While watching Jack approach the cottage, Paul was distracted by a movement on the mountain to his left. Glancing in that direction, he could scarcely

believe his eyes. A man was actually descending the almost sheer face of the mountain, just beyond the landslide!

"Come here and look," Paul whispered urgently, his eyes wide open. "I know you will not believe me, but there is a man coming straight down the mountain!"

Supported by ropes securely fixed near the top, the man was descending at considerable speed, deftly using his feet and hands, so was clearly an accomplished mountaineer. What looked like a small case was strapped to his back.

"He'll see Jack," declared Nora in dismay. "He can't

fail to!"

"No he won't," said Mike reassuringly. "For one thing, he's facing the mountain and, for another, he's busy concentrating on what he's doing. So *that's* how people enter the Secret Valley despite the pass being blocked. They're skilled mountaineers. Very clever."

As soon as he was at the foot of the mountain, the man wasted no time in removing the rope and changing his footwear before striding towards the old cottage. Although they could not see the track that had once linked the two passes, the children realised that there must be a path, as the man was walking in a fairly straight line instead of having to dodge various obstacles.

"There's the first man coming to meet him," said Paul pointing. "And look, there's Jack going into the ruin. He doesn't know another person is coming. What shall we do? We must warn him."

"It would be foolish to show ourselves," replied Peggy. "There can't be much to see in the old building, so Jack will be out in a few moments and he won't just walk out into the open. Look, the two men are about to meet."

When they did meet, they exchanged a few words before continuing on their different ways. In silence, the children watched as the second man approached the cottage. Almost at once, to their consternation, a woman appeared, having apparently come from the far end of the valley.

"Look!" yelled Mike. "Another person – a woman this time. However will Jack get away?"

The four were now convinced Jack would be spotted

as it was unlikely he could hide in such a small building. In silence they watched the two people go into the ruin, expecting to see Jack led out. For a while, nothing happened, until Jack dashed out of the cottage at full speed and dived down onto the ground.

Almost immediately, the two adults appeared, searching the outside of the ruin, the woman eventually approaching where Jack was hiding. Then, to the amazement of the watching children, the woman leapt backwards and almost ran to the bewildered man.

"Whatever's the matter with her?" asked Peggy in surprise. "What caused her to run? Did Jack make her jump?"

"No, or the man would have rushed to grab him," replied Mike. "Weird. Well, they've gone back into the cottage now. Let's hope Jack returns with some news. What's the first man doing?"

Having reached the base of the mountain, the first man was adjusting the rope. He tugged on it a few times, presumably to make sure it was secure, and began to climb up the sheer face of the mountain using some sort of a pulley to assist him. It was clearly much harder going up the mountain than descending it. The children watched in awe as he fearlessly used the smallest of hand and footholds. So intrigued were they by his progress that they didn't realise they could be seen until it suddenly dawned on Peggy.

"Get down, everyone!" she said urgently. "If he looks this way he'll see us as clearly as we can see him. Get back on the platform under the overhanging cliff. I'm going to meet Jack and warn him about the man on the mountain."

Still unable to make out the platform, Jack continued towards the waterfall. Reaching it, he scrambled up alongside looking for Mike, Nora and Paul but, instead, was surprised to find Peggy slithering down.

"Jack! Thank goodness you're all right!" she said at once. "We've just seen a man climbing the mountain! If we keep close to the waterfall he won't be able to see us. Quick! He must be near the top by now!"

Although out of breath, Jack nevertheless hurried to see the mountaineer for himself. He and Peggy reached the platform just in time to watch him reach the summit where he disappeared from sight.

"That's the man we saw earlier," explained Mike. "The second one came down the mountain face and met a woman from the other end of the valley. We were terrified they'd catch you in the old cottage."

"They almost did," said Jack grimly. "Just listen to my story."

He told the others how he had recognised the first man as being the guard, Konstantin, who had spoken to them near the landslide. They listened entranced as he informed them of the underground room, explaining his intention to return there with a torch, hopefully to retrieve the stolen plans.

"And there may well be other items of interest to the Government of Baronia in there," he added.

"Therefore I shall come with you," declared Paul at once. "I am a Prince of Baronia so I must do something useful for my country."

"You can't come down to the room with me as it

will be too dangerous for you," stated Jack firmly, patting the prince on the back. "But you can certainly come as a lookout so you can warn me if anybody approaches."

How the others roared with laughter when Jack described the toad frightening the woman and realised that was what they had witnessed. "It was just as well, as she was about to tread on me," he added, grinning. "Now we know why that unpleasant guard, Konstantin, warned us to stay on our side of the valley. He was afraid we might see him on the mountainside."

"I jolly well did!" stated Nora emphatically. "And *you* four didn't believe me!"

"That guard is a traitor!" snapped a furious Paul. "That is why the plans were so easily stolen." He stopped suddenly, putting his head on one side. "Listen. Whatever could that be?"

A loud roaring noise passing overhead made them all duck down. It was an aeroplane! It flew across in front of them as it dipped down into the Secret Valley, keeping close to the sides of the mountains.

"Quick, it's probably searching for us. Wave where we can be seen!" ordered Jack, rushing to the front of the platform and squeezing as quickly as possible between the rocks. The others followed, but by the time they were clear of the overhanging cliff, the plane had completely circled the little valley.

"Drat, it would come while we were up here on the platform hidden from view!" exclaimed Mike in annoyance. He continued waving, but it was too late.

The disappointed children could only watch in

dismay as the plane flew back over the mountain and away from the Secret Valley.

The Underground Room

As silence returned to the valley, five very despondent children looked disbelievingly at each other.

"That was a terrible mistake, being up there," muttered Jack angrily as they perched on rocks. "I know we're hiding from possibly dangerous people, but we could have been ready for the plane. After all, we guessed it would fly over the valley."

"Won't they search for us again?" asked Nora fearfully. "We can't stay here for ever."

"Of course they will when there's no sign of us near our tents," said Mike reassuringly. "Mind you, the tents may have blown across the valley in last night's storm. Still, our boat will be seen."

"The boat could have drifted across the lake if the storm cast it adrift," said Jack mournfully. "There's a good chance they're searching for us in completely the wrong place and it was pure chance the plane came over here."

"And do not forget they believe nobody can enter the Secret Valley," added Paul shrugging his shoulders in despair. "They will know we could not possibly climb up the high mountains that side then come down on this one."

"They will not give up searching, believe me,"

declared Peggy reassuringly. "Our parents are just over the mountain and we have a Prince of Baronia with us. They'll be back all right, and we must be ready for them next time."

"The man and woman seem to have disappeared," said Mike looking down the mountain. "They obviously hid when the plane arrived which shows they're up to no good. Well, I don't know about you, but I'm feeling hungry so why don't we have something to eat? If we have a meal nearer the waterfall, we can wave to the plane if it returns."

They found an enclosed area near the fall where they could keep watch without being seen themselves and where they would be in full view of any aircraft flying overhead. As they were all feeling hungry, they ate steadily, saying little.

The meal over, they sat on rocks, sheltered from the hot sunshine, deciding what to do for the best. While gazing at a fairly grassy area to the right of the lake, an idea gradually entered Peggy's head. In fact, she nearly fell off her rock, so eager was she to convey her thoughts to the others.

"See that grassy area down there?" she said, pointing excitedly. "When we were down by the lake I noticed plenty of big stones nearby. Why don't we spell the word HELP using stones? It will be seen from the air even if we're out of sight. As the enemy seem to stay on the other side of the lake, they won't notice it."

"Now that sounds an excellent idea," agreed Mike. "Well done, Peggy. Yes, there are loads of stones lying about. You can see them from here."

"Don't get me wrong – although I like the idea very much, there is one big problem," observed Jack, looking back and forth across the lake. "While we're hunting for stones, we'll be in the open and in full view of anybody on the other side of the lake, as there are plenty of spaces between the large boulders scattered about. And we'd be spotted at once by anyone on top of the mountain, or even on the mountainside."

"Surely it's a risk worth taking," stated Peggy, not liking the thought of her idea coming to nothing. "We've got to do all we can to attract the attention of an aircraft. It's the only way we'll escape from the Secret Valley."

"And don't forget, Jack, our food supply will run out tomorrow," added Mike. "We can't expect to find a cow and hens like we did on our secret island."

"I must inform you that HELP does not mean anything in Baronian," said Paul solemnly, to everyone's dismay. "Our word is very long and would need plenty of stones."

"That's a point," said Jack. "The word has to be understood by *anyone* flying over." He thought for a moment then blurted out, "I know! We'll do what Peggy suggests, but using SOS instead. Everybody understands SOS. It's only three letters and it reads the same either way up."

"The sooner we do this the better," declared Mike. "So what are our plans for the afternoon? When the coast is clear, do we spell SOS or do you still intend going to the underground room?"

"As soon as the man and woman leave the ruin – if they're still in there – I'm going to the underground

91

room to try to find the stolen plans, or any information for that matter," stated Jack, standing up. "You can go to the clearing and I'll join you as soon as possible."

"I'm going down to the cottage with you, Jack," said Paul at once. "You promised, remember?"

"Yes, you can come with me, young Paul," said Jack nodding at the determined prince. "You can be my lookout. Now, while we're waiting, someone ought to be keeping a watch here."

"I'm too tired to keep watch properly," moaned Nora, yawning.

"You're too lazy you mean!" said Peggy scornfully while Nora pulled a face. "You jolly well keep watch, Nora. You take a turn as well, Paul, at least until you go down to the ruined cottage with Jack while Mike and I go to the clearing."

"Keep a close lookout for the man and woman," instructed Jack, ignoring Nora's protests. "I'm going to fetch my torch."

Jack leapt up to the passage to fetch his torch while Mike and Peggy clambered around the rocks to sit by their waterfall. Spotting Mike's bright red jersey lying on the floor, Jack had an idea and grabbed it, taking it to Nora, now conscientiously keeping an eye on the valley.

"If you see anybody while we're away, Nora, drape Mike's jersey round this bush," said Jack handing her the garment. "It should be clearly visible from the ruined cottage and from the lake. If Paul spots it, he can let me know, as I won't see it from inside the ruin. I just hope the enemy won't notice it."

"And you can wave it if a plane comes," added Paul. "I hope we can leave soon, Jack."

For some time, there was no movement from the derelict cottage. It was not until well into the afternoon that Nora noticed both the man and the woman striding along in the general direction of the nearby mountain.

"This is our chance," said Jack, as he grimly watched them. He called Mike and Peggy. "It looks like they intend climbing the mountain. I'm going into the underground room. You can go down to the lake to collect stones, but stop if either of them starts to climb."

With Paul following closely, Jack set off. High vegetation and large boulders hid the boys from the man and woman, and Jack was confident they would reach the ruin before the two began to ascend the mountain. When they came to the track, Jack looked up and down it without spotting anybody. The two adults were out of sight around the slight bend. The boys dashed to the shelter of the bushes on the other side and bobbed down. Jack searched around a bit, finding a suitable place for Paul to keep watch.

"Keep a lookout here," he said at last. "You can see both ways along the track and you've a view of the waterfall in case Nora needs to warn us about any danger. If you want to attract my attention, run round these bushes and call through the doorway. Don't go on the track."

"I would like to see the underground room too," said Paul. "Please, Jack."

"Let me search the room first," replied Jack, smiling at the eager face of the little prince. "Right. I'm off.

Keep watch carefully."

With that, Jack crept towards the cottage – not that he expected anyone to be there. He raised the flagstone and, switching on his torch, went cautiously down the steps, wondering what he would find.

Once below, he looked around in surprise. Along one side of the wall were a radio receiver and transmitter on a makeshift shelf, spare batteries and, of all things, suitcases. In a corner were mattresses and a supply of towels. Near the steps were crockery and cutlery, a metal bowl, and a good supply of basic food in tins and cartons. On a small shelf were tin-openers and a supply of small paper bags.

"They've obviously been using this room for some time," muttered Jack. "I expect they wash in the lake, thus the footprints. Now, what's in the suitcases?"

He tried to open them, but to his annoyance all except one were firmly locked. Having managed to open the fourth case, he looked aghast at rolls of film and pages of notes and diagrams within. There was no way of knowing whether these were plans, as he could not understand the words. However, it was clear the films had not yet been exposed so, one by one, he pulled them out of their containers, rendering them useless.

Shutting the case, Jack's attention was attracted by an object beside the stairs. "Now, what's that? Yet another case?"

It was indeed another case – smaller and more solid looking. Jack lifted it up, amazed at its weight. Expecting it to be locked he was surprised to find it opened easily and he gasped at its contents. Inside were a camera, a

long-range lens, cans of film with wording on that he did not understand and, to his delight, what looked like the packet the man had held earlier.

"Phew!" he said. "This proves they're spying. I bet this has been put by the stairs to be collected later, so *I'll* take it. It's not stealing because we're convinced these people are criminals. Gosh, it's heavy. Whatever's in the packet? More than just papers, surely!"

He was about to mount the steps when a thought occurred to him. "We're going to be short of food soon. I'll put some tins and cartons in one of those bags. I'd better take a tin-opener as well. Paul can carry the bag back to the platform while I bring the case."

He quickly filled a bag then awkwardly lugged it and the heavy case up the steps. Remembering his promise to Paul, he reluctantly put the case and bag down and darted through the doorway to Paul's hiding place.

"You can have a quick look in the underground room," he said, checking there was no signal from Nora. "This way."

The prince followed Jack into the ruin, his eyes lighting up on seeing the raised flagstone. Almost tumbling down the steps with excitement, he looked around the room in amazement.

"What is this thing here?" he enquired, spotting the transmitter. "Is it a radio?"

"Sort of," replied Jack, shining his torch on it. "It sends and receives messages – like the one Pilescu has. Are these words in Baronian?"

"No, they are not!" snapped Paul angrily. "They're Maldonian! They use this thing to pass on information about Baronia. Well they will not use it anymore!"

Before Jack could stop him, the furious prince pushed the transmitter off the shelf. As it landed on the floor with a crash, switches and other parts flew off in all directions and wires jumped out of their sockets. A satisfied look now spread over Paul's face.

"Now they will not radio any more secret information!" he declared triumphantly. He bent down to pick up something else that had fallen from the shelf. A pair of field glasses!

"We must leave this room immediately," said Jack urgently. "Wait, let's see if we can do something to the shelf. There's a chance whoever finds this will think it simply gave way under the weight of the transmitter – but I doubt it. They'll know someone's been here!"

Paul half-heartedly helped Jack shift the shelf, which was firmly attached to the wall. They made it slope a little, although not enough to have caused the transmitter to fall. While they were doing this, a noise made both boys stand motionless and look at each other. It was the unmistakable sound of an aeroplane.

"Quick, get up top!" yelled Jack, pushing the young prince to the steps. "The plane's back! Let's not miss it again. And take the glasses with you."

Unfortunately, in his haste, Paul missed his footing. He slipped down the steps, landing on Jack, who lost his grip and fell. At once he was on his feet again and pushed past the younger boy as he leapt up the steps into the room above. Dashing outside the ruin, he waved violently. It was too late! For the second time that day, the plane disappeared over the mountains.

A sorrowful Paul appeared, rubbing his leg. He looked at the mountain tops then towards the waterfall, which made him look aghast. He grabbed hold of Jack's arm, a terrified look on his face.

And no wonder! The red jersey could just be seen draped around a bush on the mountainside and, worse, voices could be heard not far from the cottage...

Plenty of Excitement

As soon as Jack and Paul had set off for the underground room, Peggy and Mike hurried down the mountainside to the grassy area beside of the lake.

"Jack's right – we are very exposed out here," observed Mike once they were nearing the lake. "We'll have to be extremely careful while we collect enough stones for the SOS. The trouble is, if that man and woman climb the mountain, one of them is bound to spot us."

"I think the best thing to do is gather stones where all those boulders will hide us, then pile them up as close as possible to the area of grass before making the letters," suggested Peggy thoughtfully. She glanced up the mountainside towards Nora. "I hope Nora keeps a careful watch. That was a good idea of Jack's to drape your jersey over the bush as a danger signal. We'll easily notice it from here."

"As long as we keep looking in Nora's direction," warned Mike as they began to pick up some large stones. "Let's make three piles, one for each letter, as close to the grassy clearing as possible, yet where we can't easily be seen. If we do that, it won't take us too long to spell out SOS. In any case, Jack and Paul will join us soon. You know, I've lost track of where the ruined cottage is."

"Good job," said Peggy depositing more stones on the pile. "If we could see the ruin it would mean we might be spotted by those two walking towards the mountain – assuming that's where they're going. Look Mike, I think we'll need much larger stones than the ones we've found so far. It'll take *ages* to make readable letters with these small ones."

The two now began to be more selective in their choice of stones as both agreed that small ones would not be noticed from a fast-moving plane. This took far more time as there were not as many large ones scattered about. It was tough work lugging heavy stones in the heat, but gradually the three piles increased in size.

"Should we need to hide, there's a gap between those two long boulders over there," said Peggy nodding towards the edge of the grassy area. "It seems to go back some way and is covered with huge leaves."

"Talking of hiding, I'm surprised there's no signal from Nora," remarked Mike who had repeatedly looked up the mountain to where he knew his twin sister was keeping watch. "After all, the man and woman will have reached the base of the mountain by now. In fact, they've had time to climb to the very top."

"You're right," agreed Peggy, wiping her brow. "I hope she hasn't dropped off to sleep."

Nora was, in fact, wide awake and keeping a close watch on the man and the woman who, having reached the base of the mountain, made no attempt to climb it. They perched on a couple of rocks and kept glancing up towards the top as though expecting someone to come down.

"What on earth are they waiting for?" Nora asked herself. "Perhaps somebody's going to join them from our valley – maybe from the airbase."

She had a busy time watching the two grown ups, keeping a lookout for Jack and Paul who were out of sight, and being ready to warn Peggy and Mike to hide should anyone appear at the top of the mountain. Then a nasty thought occurred to her.

"If somebody else does climb over the mountain before I notice them, they will spot Peggy and Mike when they start forming the letters. I must have that jersey ready."

She spread the bright red garment out on the ground so that she could drape it around the bush in an instant if danger threatened, as she felt convinced it would. Wondering what Jack and Paul were doing, she glanced in their direction and opened her mouth in shock. Beyond the ruin was a definite movement on the track. Nora shielded her eyes from the sun and, there was no mistaking it, at least two more people were approaching from the far end of the valley. They would soon reach the derelict cottage where Jack and Paul were.

As quickly as possible, she draped the jersey around the bush, making certain that it faced the ruin. It would also face whoever was coming along the track, although hopefully they would not take any notice of it as they were further away. One of the sleeves kept drooping so, knowing some of the food packets had been tied up with string, Nora quickly made her way up to the platform and into the passage, terrified that Jack and Paul would not notice the danger signal in time.

It was while she was rummaging in the food bag that the plane returned! As on the previous occasion, it swooped down into the valley opposite the platform before circling round, following the base of the mountains. There was nothing Nora could do to attract its attention, although she hoped and prayed someone on board might notice the jersey. She hurried to a position in the open, but the plane was now skirting the mountains on the other side of the valley before flying over them and disappearing from view.

Poor Nora was close to tears, wondering why Peggy and Mike hadn't waved at the plane. Seeing two heads appearing from among the thick vegetation, she realised why. They had taken heed of the red jersey and had hidden.

She cautiously peered down to see where the man and woman had got to and spotted them coming out from between a couple of large rocks. Again they looked towards the top of the mountain and the woman suddenly gave a brief wave. Nora also glanced at the mountain top, expecting to see someone coming down. However, this time there was a large package being lowered on the rope. Whoever was on top of the mountain remained out of sight.

Watching the woman untie the package Nora remembered the two people she had seen approaching from the far end of the valley. To her horror, they were almost at the ruined cottage. Where *were* Jack and Paul?

Having heard the approaching voices, the two boys stood rooted to the spot for a brief moment. Then, in haste, Jack dragged a startled Paul to the rearmost room of the cottage where he lifted him through the glassless window. He hurriedly went back to fetch the case and bag of food, following the prince through the window. Safely on the ground, he quickly bobbed down, indicating to Paul not to make a sound.

The boys heard two people enter the next room, which was the old kitchen. Jack now began to feel very alarmed, as the broken transmitter was bound to be noticed at any moment and an immediate search would almost certainly begin. To move would be to make a noise so they had to wait until the flagstone was raised.

However, for some reason, the two men remained in the kitchen talking. Paul listened intently. They were speaking Maldonian, a language he could just about understand. After a while, he turned to Jack and whispered to him, knowing he would not be heard by the men who were now talking loudly and laughing.

"One of the men, Ivanu, has come for a case with a camera, the latest photos of the new plane and, listen to this, a part from the plane!" exclaimed Paul, an angry look on his face. "The other one, I think his name's Nikitu – he's the one with the deep and loud voice – will go up the mountain as soon as it's dark to collect more information about the airbase from Konstantin, who will leave a bag hidden in the usual place on the mountain top. He will take films with him for Konstantin's camera. The guard Konstantin is a traitor. How dare they do these things!"

"Shhh!" said Jack at once, as the furious little prince was raising his voice. "I know you're angry. So am I, but look. I bet this is Ivanu's case. If so, we've probably

recovered the stolen engine part. I thought the packet was heavy. Now keep your voice down and tell me what else they said."

"They are worried about the plane flying over the valley twice," explained Paul, "and they will send a message about this as soon as Kristina returns with any information she has been given today. I do not know who she is."

"I expect it's that woman who is not particularly fond of toads," observed Jack with a wry smile. "If they're puzzled by the plane, it means they are unaware of any missing children. Did they say anything else of importance?"

"No, they started talking about what they would do with the money they would be given for all the information they had collected," replied Paul, still looking angry. "Jack, we must find a way of telling someone about these spies."

"If the letters SOS had been in position by the lake, they would have been seen by the people in the aeroplane," whispered Jack. "I don't think there was time to make the letters so they must now be an absolute priority. It was great idea of Peggy's and right now we need to get over to the other side of the lake and help her and Mike."

"Do you think the other three waved to the plane?" asked Paul. "Perhaps they did and we'll be rescued."

"It depends on when Nora displayed the jersey," answered Jack. "If they noticed it before the plane arrived, they would have been hidden. We can only hope. Come on. Carry this bag of tins of food and follow me. I'll carry this heavy case. Whatever you do, *don't* tread on any branches or twigs."

Bending low, Jack led Paul alongside the wall of the

cottage, soon reaching an overgrown garden. Hearing more raucous laughter from inside the cottage, Jack indicated that they should run into the outbuilding at the end of the garden and hide there while they checked to see if the coast was clear.

"The jersey is still on the bush," said Paul, gazing round the door at the mountainside. "Do you think someone else is coming?"

"I don't know and I'm not going to guess," Jack replied curtly. "At the moment I can't see anybody on the track in either direction, so we'll cross it a bit further down. Come on."

They hurriedly left the old building and, negotiating more boulders, reached a spot where, on the other side of the track, there seemed to be a somewhat overgrown path. The important thing was that it seemed to lead to the lake.

"When I give the order, run across the track as fast as possible to that path, if it *is* a path," instructed Jack peering round the boulder. He quickly bobbed back. "No, wait a moment. I can see one of the men standing on the track, waving. Somebody must be coming. Whoever is it *this* time?"

Jack waited a short while before again looking cautiously around the boulder. He was just in time to spot the same woman he had seen earlier greet the man. A short distance behind her was the man with the brown beard. Soon all three were talking earnestly outside the cottage.

"Kristina and her friend have come back for some reason and are talking to one of the men," said Jack.

"I wonder why neither of them climbed the mountain – unless they're worried about the plane coming over again. Any moment now they'll go into the old cottage."

"And she'll want to use the transmitter to send more information about Baronia," declared Paul, a smug smile spreading over his face. "Well, I am pleased to say she will have a very nasty surprise."

"So will we if we remain here," muttered Jack. "Now we know why the jersey is still in place. Nora must have seen Kristina and the man returning along the track. Get ready to run as I'm going to have another look."

He was just creeping around the boulder to have a good view along the track when furious shouting was heard from inside the derelict cottage. One of the voices was clearly the woman's so Jack knew Kristina had now entered the underground room with the intention of using the transmitter.

"They've obviously been down below and seen the damage so run as fast as you can across to that path, Paul," ordered Jack. "And don't stop when you get there. Keep moving!"

The young prince sped across the track, making his way as best he could along the very much overgrown path. Jack followed at once, but before he reached the other side he tripped on a rut in the track. Although he didn't fall down he did drop the precious case. He was hurriedly picking it up when one of the men, a huge ape-like figure, came on to the track and gave a loud bellow.

He had spotted Jack!

The Boys Are Discovered!

Meanwhile, down beside the lake Mike and Peggy had been busy gathering stones when Peggy suddenly spotted the jersey draped over the bush.

"The danger signal!" she exclaimed, grabbing hold of her brother. "It probably means those two people are climbing up the mountain. They'll have an uninterrupted view of us down here if we don't hide."

"Let's go and hide among those long boulders where we won't be seen by anyone on the mountain," said Mike dropping the stone he had just picked up. "Hurry! Nora might have spotted someone coming down the mountain – someone who could see us right now."

Dashing over to the boulders they had noticed earlier, they squeezed some way between them, startling some toads that hopped away in disgust at having their home invaded by uninvited visitors. Surprisingly, there were other boulders that were set at right angles, forming a corner beyond which the space rapidly increased the further they went in.

"It's a great hiding place, but the trouble is we can't see what's going on from here," moaned Peggy ducking beneath the leafy vegetation which formed a roof. "I wonder *why* Nora signalled."

"It's best we stay hidden," replied Mike earnestly.

"These leaves conceal us perfectly from anyone on the mountain or by the lake. I hope Paul has spotted the jersey and warned Jack."

Unfortunately, it was while they were squatting in their hiding place that the plane returned, flying over the Secret Valley. Brother and sister listened aghast, unable to stand up, let alone wave. Although they eased their way back outside to signal as quickly as possible, they were too late. There was the plane – already heading back over the mountains.

"I wonder if anyone in the plane noticed the jersey," said Mike as they emerged from their cover. He looked up to the platform. "I doubt it. Look, it's facing downwards."

"The fact that the jersey's still there means we should remain hidden," pointed out Peggy. "Do keep down, Mike."

"Don't worry, the enemy will have hidden as soon as they heard the plane," replied Mike, moving back to the boulders. "Actually, I hope there *was* someone on the mountain as he'd have been seen and his presence reported. An investigation would certainly take place."

They remained where they were for some time, unable to collect more stones in case they were noticed by the enemy until, to her surprise, Peggy's sharp ears heard shouting from the other side of the lake.

"Listen, Mike!" she said urgently. "Something serious must have happened for that man to bellow like that. I do hope Jack and Paul haven't been caught."

"I'm jolly well going to find out," said Mike, ignoring his sister's pleas to remain with her. "You make your

109

way up to Nora. Tell her to remove the jersey in case the enemy spots it and sees where we're hiding. I'll work my way round this side of the lake. The shouting is coming from the other side – probably where the ruined cottage is. We must find out if anything has happened to Jack and Paul."

At that very moment, Jack and Paul were creeping towards the water while the furious bellowing continued. Realising that the path they were using would be noticed and almost certainly followed, Jack led Paul away from it, dodging boulders and thick undergrowth in their attempt to reach the lake. Suddenly, there was the sparkling water, just a short distance ahead. Stopping to listen, Jack heard the ominous sound of feet trampling down vegetation not far away. The pursuer was much too close for comfort.

"Run to the left!" hissed Jack picking up a large stone which he hurled with all his might in the opposite direction. It clattered noisily off two rocks before falling into the undergrowth. "Hopefully they'll think we're over there. Now we must keep at least one rock or boulder between us and the water or we'll be exposed to anyone by the lake."

These words were hardly out of his mouth when he heard shouting coming from where the stone had landed. Parting some leaves, Jack peered between them and saw the woman beside the water looking up and down the shore.

"Don't move at all, Paul," said Jack, hardly daring to breathe. "That woman Kristina's standing on the shore. She's obviously watching for any sign of movement in the undergrowth as she's standing quite still."

"I hope a toad jumps at her," said Paul, giggling. "Then she will not keep still. She might even fall in the water."

"No such luck," said Jack with a grin. He clutched Paul by the arm. "Look, there's one of the men, further along the shore. Let me have the glasses a moment."

He took the field glasses from Paul and, from the shelter of the leafy bush, focused first on the mountain used by the enemy, then slowly surveyed the shore of the lake. Finally he looked towards the waterfall just in time to see the jersey being removed from the bush.

"Thank goodness, Nora's removing the jersey," he declared. "I was beginning to fear someone would notice it. There's nobody on the other side of the lake... Oh no, the man's coming in this direction! Let's move away from the water."

They crept onwards, making slow progress as the undergrowth grew thicker. Concerned that they might get lost, Jack soon stopped and began to climb on to a rock. Almost immediately he fell flat, a finger to his mouth indicating for silence. Nearby was the sound of feet trampling down the undergrowth and the man with the brown beard could be spotted between the leaves. He stopped and shouted. There was a distant reply from Kristina. The man muttered angrily to himself before turning back.

"He said there are no footprints by the water and no way into the bushes," explained Paul. "Kristina called him Georgi and told him to push into the bushes as soon as there's a gap."

"He'll walk into us!" exclaimed Jack. He looked around. There was no way forward and to retreat would mean confronting Georgi. "Climb over this rock. Quick!"

The boys had scarcely tumbled to the ground on the other side of the rock when Georgi, pushing wildly through the undergrowth, reached the spot where they had been hiding a few moments earlier. He called to Kristina. In a concerned whisper, Paul translated that the man had noticed trampled vegetation which meant someone had hidden there. To their horror, the man climbed onto the rock. Feeling Paul tremble, Jack patted him gently. Both boys pressed their backs against the rock, hoping Georgi would not peer directly over the edge.

He slowly moved across the flat top of the rock, looking for signs of movement in the vegetation or between boulders, little knowing that two scared boys were just below him. One more step and he would see them! He was just taking this step when there was a shout from another man. To the boys' relief, Georgi turned and leapt down on the opposite side to where they were hiding.

Jack remained still for some time before cautiously clambering back on to the rock. "Drat! We're no closer to the waterfall than we were last time we stopped!" he exclaimed, feeling annoyed as he looked around. "We've almost gone around in a circle. We'll have to risk approaching the water to find a landmark. This undergrowth is unbearably dense."

The boys found it more and more difficult to reach

the water although, as Jack pointed out, this made it equally hard for anyone to find them. Eventually they emerged from a huge bush to find themselves not far from the shore of the lake. More importantly, the shouting was more distant. Suddenly Paul's sharp ears heard a movement not far ahead. He grabbed hold of Jack. "Listen, someone is coming and is quite close."

Again they remained motionless. The sound of feet trampling through vegetation and stones being moved meant someone was approaching. They held their breath, wondering who could have come round the lake so swiftly. Jack held Paul's hand, ready to run, as a weary figure emerged from behind a leafy bush.

It was Mike!

"Gosh, it's *you*, Mike!" declared Jack in amazement and relief. "What on earth are you doing? How did you find us? Those people know someone has been in their underground room and are searching for us. It's lucky you weren't spotted."

"So *that's* what the shouting was about," said Mike, sitting on a rock. "For an awful moment, we thought you'd been captured. What's in the bag and case – and where did you get those glasses from, Paul?"

"We'll tell the full story later," answered Jack. "The important thing is that the spies had a radio transmitter which has been destroyed by His Royal Highness here, so you can guess the mood they're in. They know strangers are about, although I think they only had a glimpse of me when I tripped on the track. Listen, there's more shouting – and it's getting closer. Where's Peggy?"

"Gone back to join Nora," replied Mike, "and the sooner we're back with them the better."

"Did you wave to the plane?" asked Paul hopefully.

"No, we were hiding because of the red jersey," said Mike pulling a face. "What about you?"

"We were in the underground room when we heard the plane," explained Jack beginning to move between more boulders. "Mind you, we couldn't have waved in the open as two more men had appeared from somewhere. Did you have time to make any of the SOS sign?"

"We gathered plenty of stones, but no, we didn't have time to form the letters, worse luck!" answered a despondent Mike, following Jack and Paul. "I'll take that bag, Paul. How are we going to finish the job with these people in the valley? And why are there so many of them?"

"We know that at least one of the men, the so-called guard Konstantin, the miserable one who spoke to us, is able to carry information up the mountain from the airbase without arousing suspicion," replied Jack. "Others transmit information by radio or carry it through the Secret Valley to – guess where. Maldonia! The country on the other side of those mountains."

"Spies and traitors!" cried Paul, his temper flaring up. "We must catch them!"

"At the moment it's more likely they'll catch *us*," said Mike cynically. "Let me take the lead, Jack. I think I remember the way back."

The three ploughed their way with some difficulty through undergrowth that had been largely undisturbed for many years. Mike followed the narrow path he had made through the vegetation, stopping every so often to check they were approaching the waterfall which was their only guide, as the mountain tops all looked the same. Suddenly they came upon the clearing where they had planned to form the letters SOS.

"Let's make the letters now," said Paul, carelessly wandering out into the open place. "Where are the stones you collected, Mike?"

Before Mike could answer, there was a yell from around the lake. Paul had been spotted and froze on the spot! Jack had to leave the shelter of the boulders to drag him back. Kristina and one of the men now began running along the shore. Soon another man appeared from near the ruined cottage and, joining in the shouting, ran quickly round the other side of the lake.

"Wherever are we going to hide?" asked Jack looking round in despair. "We'll never reach our platform without giving away our hiding place."

Mike thought for a moment then cried, "Follow me! I know the very place." Praying that he was going in the right direction, he made for the vegetation-covered boulders where he and Peggy had hidden a short while earlier. Round a bush he darted, jumped over a rock and, yes, there were the boulders ahead. If only he and the others could all squeeze between them before the enemy could spot them!

Saying nothing, he breathlessly dived under the covering vegetation and wriggled as quickly as possible between the boulders, desperately clinging to the bag of food. Paul followed and, being smaller, easily kept right behind Mike. Bringing up the rear, Jack entered the narrow space feet first so that he would know if the hiding place had been spotted and to make it easier for him to drag the weighty case.

Mike and Paul were now in the wider section round the corner. After passing the case to the others, Jack crawled back to the entrance to listen. His heart was pounding with fear as the yelling was very close indeed. In fact, someone was so close that a shadow fell across the gap between the boulders.

Holding his breath fearfully, Jack wriggled back to the other two. The look on his face was enough to make them remain silent and keep as still as possible. Paul even started holding his breath, while their hearts almost stopped beating as one of the men had clearly noticed the gap between the boulders. And what's more, he began to crawl inside it!

The Enemy on the Trail

The boys remained frozen with fear. They heard the man puffing heavily while muttering to himself as he slowly squeezed through the gap between the boulders. He paused for a moment. The boys were terrified. If he moved further forward, even just a few inches, he would certainly spot them huddled round the corner, holding their breath.

Very, very slowly, the seconds passed while, all the time, the man's breathing could be clearly heard. There came a yell from one of the other men, causing him to remain still while he listened. The horrified boys saw his outstretched hand come into view then, saying something to himself, he retreated.

The boys let out huge sighs of relief, realising what a narrow escape they had just had. They all wiped the perspiration from their brows.

"The shouting was about something they saw near a stone wall not far from where we are," explained Paul. "Luckily the man was telling himself that nobody could hide further along between the boulders as the gap became too narrow. Good job he stopped where he did or he would have seen that bag of food. I just could not move it."

"I really thought he would hear our hearts pounding,"

said Jack, now taking deep breaths. "Well, I'll crawl to the entrance to see where those people are now. We've got to reach the platform. We can't have the girls up there and us down here, especially as it's obvious we're going to have to spend the night in the Secret Valley."

"It's not a very secret one with all these people around," moaned Mike. "How on earth do we climb up to our platform without being noticed?"

"As soon as the enemy move – from here and, from what Paul has told us, they're moving over to a stone wall – we should be able to make our way up alongside the waterfall," answered Jack. "Peggy told me that there are plenty of rocks and boulders which will hide us all the way up on the left side. We'll just have to be careful crossing the fall itself. She said we should do this once we're on a level with our platform. Now if you hear any shouting, Paul, please translate."

Paul listened intently as he tried to make out what was being said. Trying not to giggle at the look of amazement on the faces of a couple of toads who had come leaping along, he was able to eventually inform the others that the men would approach the wall from different sides. Kristina intended to keep watch from on top of a flat rock.

"I remember noticing the wall leading from what appeared to be an old farmhouse," recalled Mike. "It's at the foot of the mountain well to the left of our platform viewed from here, so completely out of our way. Can you see Kristina, Jack? If not, I reckon we could risk dashing over to the bottom of the waterfall."

Jack eased himself out of the hiding place and, slowly

standing up, peered around. At first he could see nobody then, turning the other way, he received a shock – there was Kristina standing on a rock. He ducked, despite the fact she was facing the mountain, knowing she could turn round at any moment and see him.

"If we crawl on all fours we should be able to reach the bottom of the fall," Jack said as he returned for the precious case. Paul looked at him questioningly. "Ah, 'on all fours' means crawling like a dog, Paul. The men are out of sight, presumably by the farmhouse, and Kristina is watching from a rock. She looks just like a statue."

"So I hope a toad jumps at her!" declared Paul, almost spitting out the words as he followed Jack into the open air. "Then she won't keep still like a statue. She will fall off the rock and hurt herself. And I shall be so, so pleased."

"You and those toads!" laughed Jack. "That's the second time you've wished a toad would make Kristina tumble. Mind you, it would be rather funny. Now come on, get down on all fours. See that light coloured rock over there near the foot of the falls? That's what we'll make for. Ready? Let's go, and no talking till we're there!"

Like three prowling animals the boys crawled towards the rock that Jack had indicated. It was not very easy moving on all fours, as stones were quite painful to bare knees. However, hearing more shouting spurred them on. What a relief it was to reach the rock, where they remained in a crouching position.

"At all costs we must stay hidden from view as we

climb up beside the water," said Mike, gazing upwards. "I do hope Kristina doesn't spot us. I can't actually see her. She's certainly not standing on a rock any more."

"Don't forget the men searching near that old stone wall," warned Jack. "We don't know exactly where they are so we must take utmost care. Lead the way, Mike, and remember to keep to the left of the fall. Make certain there is always a boulder or large stone between us and the enemy in the valley."

Mike cautiously led the way, followed by Paul who was longing to use the field glasses to find out where Kristina and the men were. Jack kept peering behind, fearing there was someone following them, yet knowing it was just his imagination. Reaching their pool in the rocks, they longed to cool down in it, but had to press onwards and upwards.

Suddenly they were surprised to hear a voice calling them from above. It was Nora!

"There are people down there on the right near an old farmhouse at the foot of the mountain," she said, just making herself heard above the sound of the water. "They keep looking all around so be careful when you cross the fall."

"Don't show yourself, whatever you do, Nora," replied Jack before calling up to Mike. "Stop when you're level with the platform, Mike. We're going to have to be extra careful crossing because the stones could well be slippery. The water is moving pretty swiftly after last night's rain."

Mike continued upwards for a few paces, preparing to cross the fall. Before he could do so, Jack gave a yell, making him jump. "Stop, Mike! Wait, I've just thought of something. We must take off our shoes."

"Whatever for?" asked Mike in surprise. "The less we have to carry, the better."

"If we cross wearing shoes, we're going to leave wet prints on the stones and rocks on the other side and the prints will lead to our hiding place," replied Jack. "Once we've crossed, we can put our shoes back on. Even though I don't suppose for one moment anyone will search up here, we mustn't take anything for granted. Go on, Mike."

After removing his shoes, Mike held his breath before inching his way across the water, knowing that anybody looking up at the waterfall from the valley below would almost certainly see him. Once across, he put down the bag and shoes and turned to assist Paul, who crossed quite nimbly despite having field glasses around his neck. Jack followed, using the case and his shoes to help him keep his balance. Safely across the cascading water, the three bent down to put their shoes back on.

"Phew, thank goodness we're nearly there!" said Jack, leaning against an almost round rock as he tied up his laces. Unfortunately the rock was perched precariously on a boulder and Jack's weight caused it to shift and roll. To everyone's horror, it tumbled off the boulder, somehow bounced across the waterfall and crashed noisily down the mountainside to the valley below, gathering speed as it fell.

The boys looked at each other aghast, knowing the enemy could not fail to have heard the sound of the crashing rock and, worse, would have a good idea where

it had fallen from.

"Now what are we going to do?" asked Paul fearfully. "They must have heard the rock crashing down. It was so loud. They now know where to look for us."

"Keep well down and make for the platform, Mike," ordered Jack. "It doesn't matter how slowly we have to move as we haven't far to go, so crouch or crawl if necessary. Only climb onto the platform where there's a rock to hide behind."

Not surprisingly, urgent shouts could be heard from the valley below as the enemy had indeed heard the falling rock. In fact two of the men actually spotted it tumbling before it came to rest so they knew roughly where it had come from.

Reaching the platform, the boys squeezed between the rocks and hurried back into the passage. They were greeted by two white-faced girls who looked absolutely terrified.

"We heard the rock fall off the boulder and go crashing down into the valley," said Peggy. "Two of the men actually saw it falling and pointed, so they know where it fell from. *Whatever* shall we do?"

"There's only one thing we can do and that is to remain here where we're reasonably safe," answered Jack calmly. "That rock tumbled across the waterfall so there's a chance the people down below won't realise it started falling from this side. Give me the glasses, Paul. I'm going to creep on to the platform and see what the enemy are up to. Don't worry, I'll make certain they don't spot me."

Slowly Jack crept out on to the platform and, safely

hidden between two tall rocks, focused the glasses on the scene way below. At first he saw nobody, then from behind a huge boulder appeared the huge, ape-like man who had spotted him near the cottage, followed closely by a second. They were climbing up the mountain on the other side of the waterfall.

"Two men are coming up!" exclaimed Jack in horror. "I hope we haven't left anything by our pool. I wonder where Kristina is... there she is! A bit further over from the men – and much higher."

No longer needing the glasses, Jack continued to watch. The others cautiously came on to the platform to find out what was happening. From time to time they could hear the men, who had now reached the place where the water tumbled into the pool. It seemed to Jack they were carefully searching that area, although for much of the time they were hidden from view. Every so often there were shouts heard between them and Kristina.

"They say the stone fell from where they are now," translated Paul. "No, wait. Kristina is saying the stone must have fallen from higher up. And she's right, isn't she? I hope they don't find our platform!"

"It won't mean anything to them if they do find it," said Peggy. "The worrying thing would be if they actually climbed onto it and noticed the cave and the passage. Where's that woman now, Jack? I can still hear her."

"Almost on a level with our platform," replied Jack, getting ready to move back if necessary. "Oh no. She's looking this way, although she hasn't yet crossed the fall."

At that moment she called loudly to one of the men

who came up to join her. In alarm, Paul grabbed hold of Jack. "She's telling him to cross the fall and search this side," he said. "Let's go back into the passage, Jack. We'll be safe there."

"Not if anyone sees our belongings in the entrance – and we haven't time to move everything," replied Jack. He thought for a moment. "There's no sense in us all being captured, and Paul must definitely not be caught. Take a torch and go round the first bend in the passage. I'll stay here and see what happens. If they come in here and catch me, I'll pretend I'm alone. After all, I was the one spotted by that ape of a man near the old cottage. Now go, and take the case with you."

The others reluctantly left Jack. Mike wanted to stay, but he had the sense to realise there was no point in risking getting caught too. If the men did take Jack prisoner, perhaps he and the other children would be able to rescue him. Jack found a gap between two rocks from which he could just see what was happening. Kristina and a man were talking while, to Jack's consternation, the man crossed the fall and began to approach the platform.

"Help, he's coming this way," Jack muttered to himself, his heart pounding. He crawled back into the cave-like passage and tried to squeeze into a small cranny. He was now in semi-darkness with a view out onto the platform.

He heard a loud shout, so the man was obviously very close indeed. A few moments later, silhouetted against the sky, a looming ape-like figure mounted the platform, just a few feet from the watching boy.

Paul's Great Idea

Determined to put on a brave face if caught, Jack felt his heart pounding. Keeping still, his throat dry, he heard Kristina shout followed by a loud response from the man nearby. Surprisingly, the man did not peer into the passage, instead looking all around outside. After what seemed like ages although was really less than a minute, Jack watched the figure suddenly leap off the platform.

Remaining in the shadows, the boy left his hiding place and was amazed to spot the man apparently glancing down at his feet. The reason why became obvious as Kristina, now having crossed the waterfall, was pointing to the ground.

"I bet she's pointing out their wet footprints and saying nobody could have crossed the fall recently as there are no other prints," thought Jack feeling extremely relieved. "Good job we removed our shoes before crossing the fall."

Both the man and the woman returned to the waterfall so Jack called the other children, instructing Paul to listen to try to hear what was being said. The little prince strained his ears, but the sound of the water drowned out normal conversation. However, from the foot of the mountain where another man was looking up came an unexpected shout. Kristina yelled back and the two had a brief shouted conversation. When they stopped, Paul looked up in delight.

"They were shouting in Baronian," he explained. "It's good news. They said they will have to leave the valley now as it will soon be dark."

"How very, very peculiar," remarked Jack thinking carefully.

"What's peculiar?" asked Nora. "They're going to leave the valley so we'll be able to form the SOS letters. That's great – yet you look puzzled."

"That's because I am," answered Jack. "Think about it. We've entered the Secret Valley, we've discovered their hiding place, we've removed a case containing a camera and what we think is the stolen part of the secret plane, we've destroyed their transmitter... Can you really believe they are simply going to leave the valley because it's dark?"

"You're right, Jack," agreed Peggy. "It doesn't make sense because they must be desperate to catch us. We know too much and we've ruined their plans."

"And why speak in Baronian if that isn't their language?" asked Mike, also puzzled. "Unless, of course, they assume whoever they are after is Baronian."

"You mean, they wanted us to hear them?" said Paul, his head on one side. "You do not think they will really leave the valley?"

"Of course they won't!" retorted Jack, peering down between the rocks. "They wouldn't have shouted their plans up and down the mountainside unless what they were saying wasn't true. They knew they'd be heard and hoped we'd become careless. They'll hide, wait and watch, mark my words."

"Well, we can't do anything right now, so how about having something to eat?" suggested Mike. "We haven't eaten for ages and I'm starving. What are those people doing, Jack?"

"They're going down," said Jack, using the field glasses. "They'll soon be down in the valley. Good idea about food, Mike. It's getting quite late."

"Let's eat outside," said Peggy. "It's becoming dark in here. Nobody will notice us unless they come back up the mountain. I wonder why the man didn't notice our belongings when he stood on the platform."

"For one reason, he kept looking around the mountainside," replied Jack, "and, for another, in contrast to the sunshine, the passage is extremely dark and scarcely noticeable. He must have been using the platform as a lookout place."

"I'll help you with the food, Peggy," said Mike. "I'll take over from Jack later. At least we have a new supply of food."

Most of the tins did not have illustrated labels so Paul translated the wording. The children were indeed hungry and ready for the meal which they enjoyed as the sun began to disappear over the mountain behind them casting huge, menacing shadows in the Secret Valley.

Jack watched restlessly while he ate. "Kristina and two of the men certainly look as though they intend to leave the valley – which I refuse to believe," he remarked, genuinely surprised to notice the three continuing along the track beyond the ruined cottage. "That suggests Ivanu still plans to meet Konstantin."

The meal over, Mike took a turn at keeping watch – not that he could see any movement – while the others crept about gathering as much bracken as possible for their beds. It was not easy as they had to keep bending low to remain well hidden from prying eyes in the valley, but eventually there was quite a pile of bracken and large leaves to go on top of the moss.

The shadows lengthened as darkness gradually descended, obscuring familiar landmarks. For some time the children discussed their hopeless situation, convinced that even if they went down to the valley in the early morning, somebody would be looking out for them and capture them.

Before settling down for the night, Jack decided to go back through the passage to see if there was a slim chance of clearing the fallen stones and rocks. Not surprisingly, he found it impossible to move the huge fallen rock. Any hopes of escaping that way were severely dashed.

After some time, he gloomily returned to the others. "We'll never shift those stones," he said. "In any case, there's that landslide at the far end. I think it'd be sensible to decide what to do in the morning after we've had a sleep and our minds are fresh. Right now, we're all pretty tired."

Indeed they were. Having had a restless night after the storm followed by a busy day, nobody argued with Jack's suggestion. After more chatting they lay down on their makeshift beds beneath the overhanging cliff and, one by one, dropped off to sleep. It was in the early hours of the morning when Paul was awakened by what seemed to be a light shining in his face. He sat up with a start, fearing the hiding place had been discovered.

It was only bright moonlight striking his face, so he relaxed. Rubbing his eyes, the little prince decided he wanted to look out on the Secret Valley bathed in moonlight. He crept out on to the platform, and over to the rocks. What a scary view confronted him! Everywhere, the light from the full moon cast weirdly shaped shadows, some big, others small. It was a warm night, without wind, so nothing stirred. The only sound was a soothing one, that of the waterfall tumbling gently down the mountainside.

The lake took on an eerie, almost unreal appearance, shimmering in the soft light as though behind a veil. The grassy area beside the lake was a strange dark green colour, watched over by menacing, sombre grey rocks that melted into the darkness. Paul thought of the people who used to live and work in the valley and shivered. Then, to his alarm, as tiredness and imagination gradually took hold of him, he believed he could see their ghosts moving about in the clearing down below.

Beginning to feel scared, he turned to go back to bed when an idea came into his head. He stopped and once again looked down at the clearing. Suddenly he felt wide awake. There were no ghosts down there this time. His mind ticked over. Would it be possible to carry out his idea? Should he wake Jack and tell him? As the answer to both questions was "yes", he crept back and shook Jack, whispering urgently in his ear.

"Jack, Jack, wake up, I have a great idea. Please stop grunting. Wake up!"

Jack yawned, blinked and shook his head, trying to

decide where he was and what was happening. He was amazed to find Paul shaking him and speaking excitedly.

"Whatever's the matter, Paul?" he asked. "What do you mean, you've an idea? It's the middle of the night and I'm tired. Wait till morning."

"The morning will be too late, so please come outside," begged Paul almost tugging poor Jack off his bed. "See for yourself."

Convinced he was in the middle of a weird dream, Jack reluctantly followed the prince to a corner of the platform where the still, dark, shadowy valley presented itself. Pleadingly, he looked at Paul for an explanation.

"Down there," said Paul indicating the moonlit clearing. "Tell me. What do you see?"

"You wake me up to ask me what I can see!" exclaimed Jack, sounding annoyed. "It's the grassy bit beside the lake, silly. The moonlight's shining onto it – that's why it's a funny colour."

"Yes, the moon is shining down there!" declared Paul, his eyes wide open with excitement. "Don't you understand, Jack? We can go down now and spell SOS with the stones Mike said he and Peggy have already collected. We'll be able to see by the bright light of the moon but the enemy won't see us as they are not on the mountainside."

The reason for Paul's excitement became clear to Jack. Now fully awake like Paul, he stared at the clearing and thought for a moment while Paul fixed his gaze on him.

"Paul," he replied, turning to look at the prince, "I do believe you are right. I wonder if we can find our way down the mountainside safely by moonlight. I'll wake Mike."

He went back and woke Mike, who was as surprised as Jack had been only a few minutes earlier. Soon he too was gazing in awe at the ghostly Secret Valley and immediately realised that an opportunity presented itself to spell out SOS. Quickly, he fumbled for his shoes.

The boys' excited chattering woke Nora who wondered what on earth was going on. Almost beside himself, Paul informed her of his great idea. So loudly did he speak that he woke Peggy who wanted to join the boys in the valley below.

"No, you stay here with Nora," said Jack firmly. "Going down the mountainside in the middle of the night will be risky, even with torches. It's not like daylight when we can see every rock sticking out of the ground and every cleft. Even though I can't think anyone else is about, it's better you remain here in case we're seen – or even caught. I'd really like Paul to stay with you as well."

"What!" exclaimed the indignant prince. "It was *my* idea, Jack, so *I* am definitely coming with you."

"All right, all right, Your Highness," laughed Jack. "We'll take a torch each and shine the light downwards so we can see exactly where we're placing our feet. I only hope a cloud doesn't come to obscure the moonlight. Paul, you keep between Mike and me. Off we go! We'll be as quick as we can, girls."

Jack led the way slowly and carefully across the fall and down the mountainside. Every so often their feet dislodged small stones, some of which clattered down the mountain worryingly noisily in the still night.

However, Jack convinced himself that the sound of the water would deaden the noise. At times the moonlight was so bright that they did not need their torches but, once in the shadow of a rock, torchlight was vital for safety's sake.

Reaching the valley floor safely, Mike tried to remember where they had left the piles of stones. Everything looked so strange and different in the moonlight. It was Paul who found the piles by tripping over one of them.

"Here they are," he called, picking himself up and shining his torch on the stones. "There are plenty of stones here, so we can make big letters."

"Mike and I will form a letter S each and you make the O between them," decided Jack. "Remember, we'll be out in the open so no shouting, and keep a lookout for any lights."

Mike and Paul watched Jack begin to make his S so they had an idea what size to make their letters. Fortunately there was sufficient light from the moon for the boys to start forming the three letters, although they did have to use torches when removing stones from the piles.

Up on the ledge the girls watched all this anxiously. It looked as though a strange ritual was taking place down below as the shadowy figures hurried back and forth. Nora shivered even though she knew it was only the boys. She gazed at the glistening lake, then at the far mountains silhouetted against the dark sky. She looked down again at the boys, and then across to where she knew the farmhouse was. And she gasped in horror!

Although Nora could not see the farmhouse, she could see a flashing beam of light. What's more, the beam was definitely shining in her direction. She turned to Peggy and was dismayed to find a horrified look on her sister's face too. Peggy had been looking in the other direction, at the moonlight shining on the mountain to her left, the mountain used to enter and leave the Secret Valley. There was no mistaking it – by the light of the moon, she made out a shadowy figure on the mountain. And whoever it was would be able to clearly spot the boys as he descended into the Secret Valley.

In the Middle of the Night

Down in the valley, the boys were engrossed in their work, completely unaware of either the flashing light or the person descending the mountain. The letters were slowly taking shape when both Jack and Mike realised they were running out of stones.

"Drat!" exclaimed Jack. "We daren't make the letters any smaller in case they can't be read from the air. We'll have to search for more stones. Paul needs all those on his pile."

"There are plenty more nearer the lake," answered Mike. "Peggy and I noticed them, although we didn't take any as we would have been out in the open. Let's go there."

It was tiring work looking for suitable stones in the semi-darkness, then lugging them over to the grassy area. Paul finished his letter first and went to assist Jack and Mike. Soon their mission was accomplished. Now feeling very tired, the boys perched on rocks, delighted at having completed their task but not looking forward to scrambling back up the mountainside guided by only the weak moonlight.

Despite his weariness, an idea entered Jack's head. Having removed his jersey when he had felt hot carrying stones around, he ran onto the grassy area and spread it out in the middle of Paul's letter O. "Someone in the search plane will spot it and may guess it belongs to one of us," he explained returning to the others.

"You've overlooked the fact that the enemy might also notice it," warned Mike, stifling a yawn. "Then they'll spot the SOS."

"They'll have to notice the letters anyway before they see the jersey," replied Jack. "It's a risk worth taking. I don't like the idea of having to stay up there on that platform all day tomorrow, yet we daren't leave it as I'm convinced somebody will be watching for us. The enemy know we're somewhere on this mountainside."

"So you think they'll search for us tomorrow?" asked Paul sounding worried.

"Of course! What's more, they're bound to be up and about very early," said Jack. "They'll hide somewhere close by and wait for one of us to appear."

"I feel so sleepy," said Paul rubbing his eyes. "I expect the enemy are fast asleep in their underground room."

"I shouldn't think so for one minute," retorted Mike at once. "They don't know they're up against a group of children. They probably think there are grown ups around – like themselves. As their secret room has been discovered they're not likely to be sleeping in it, are they?"

"Gosh, you're right, Mike," said Jack. "Of course they won't be in that room. No wonder Kristina and her friends walked past the cottage. They'll be somewhere else in the valley. I just hope they're not nearby."

The three looked around fearfully at the vague shapes and weird shadows surrounding them. It was not difficult to imagine hidden eyes focused on them, watching every movement. How they longed to be safely back on their platform!

"I think we'd better return to the girls before we drop off to sleep down here," said Jack, shaking his head in an effort to remain awake. He half slid off his rock. "Ready, you two?"

Mumbling and nodding their heads, Mike and Paul left their rocks, and three weary boys stumbled back towards the waterfall, now an eerie silvery ribbon on the mountainside, little realising they were being watched from above.

"We'd better be extra careful where we place our feet, as we're tired out," warned Mike. "And we're going to have to use torches, as all we can see going this way are our own shadows."

Reaching the foot of the mountain, the boys switched on their torches, shading their lights as much as possible. Taking a deep breath, Jack started to lead the way upwards.

"At least we know where to make for," said Paul looking up the mountainside. "One of the girls has switched on a torch to guide us."

"I jolly well hope they haven't 'cause it could be seen by anyone watching in the valley," said Jack at once. He glanced up the mountain and, spotting a bright beam of light over to one side, gave an urgent command. "Turn off your torches at once and keep quite still. That light is not from our platform and it's from a more powerful torch than the ones we have. Someone else is up there!"

Mike and Paul stood motionless, horrified. Jack was right! The light was well to the left of their platform. It was moving, but it was hard to tell if the person holding the torch was coming down the mountain or walking across its slope.

"Why show an obvious light in bright moonlight?" whispered a puzzled Jack. "It doesn't make sense. Whoever is up there must have seen us and yet is giving his or her position away. Something's wrong. Let's go down to more level ground in case we have to run."

Now led by Mike, the boys cautiously made their way back down to the valley, fortunately no longer in need of their torches, as they were facing the moonlight. Then, to their horror, the ray of light from the torch was aimed directly down at them!

"Quick! Hide behind that tall rock," ordered Jack, grabbing Paul by the arm. "The beam can't reach us there."

The boys rushed to the rock and waited while they got their breath back. Then Paul, who was glancing towards the lake, uttered an anguished cry and pointed. "What is that shape over by the lake? It cannot be a rock."

The other two looked towards the lake where they knew there were no rocks. There was definitely an upright silhouette near the water's edge. What could it be? They remained motionless until, to their alarm, the shape moved.

"It's one of the enemy!" exclaimed Mike, gritting his teeth. "That's why the person on the mountain deliberately showed a light. So we would turn round and be caught by whoever's down here! Listen, what's that?"

It was the sound of stones scattering down the mountainside, showing that the first person was speedily descending. Now the second one, still a dark and menacing silhouette, slowly approached like a huge gorilla, growing larger and more horrifying with each step.

"For goodness' sake make for that place where we hid yesterday afternoon, Mike," said Jack urgently. "That's if you can find it by moonlight. I know it's near the edge of the grassy area because we ran from it to the waterfall. Paul, keep close to me."

Mike disappeared around the rock, with Jack almost dragging the tired Paul not far behind. They darted between two boulders then Jack drew in his breath as he saw the silhouette over to his left, cutting across the area of grass in an attempt to get ahead of the fleeing boys.

While Mike carried on, Jack and Paul immediately swerved to run between more rocks, bending as low as possible in order not to be seen by either of their pursuers. Then they stopped to listen. For a moment there was a strange, unnerving silence. It was broken by the sound of footsteps on stones. Someone was very close, but where? It was too late to run, so Jack pulled Paul down just as a bright ray of light lit up nearby boulders. Scarcely daring to breathe, the boys kept perfectly still while the person approached.

Slowly the man passed by. As soon as it was safe, Jack led Paul back towards the grassy clearing, but again came to a sudden halt. The sound of a stone being kicked meant another person was nearby. The boys listened intently. They heard a cough and slow footsteps. Feeling frantic, as he could not tell exactly where this person was, Jack spotted two long, narrow boulders that were close together and covered with vegetation. He pushed Paul between them, telling him to move as far forwards as possible, then he followed, almost squashing the prince in his haste to get out of sight as another cough indicated the man was just a few feet away.

Jack kept a tight hold of Paul, who was half asleep, knowing that any movement would give them away. He strained his ears and heard the sound of footsteps accompanied by the sound of deep breathing. The man stopped. Jack held his breath, dreading that his feet were showing. He felt the vegetation move and expected any moment to be dragged out, feet first.

The person moved away. Suddenly, Jack realised where they were. By pure good fortune they had found the very place they were looking for – their hiding place from the day before. He told Paul, who started to relax a little until a nasty thought occurred to him.

"Jack, this means that if *we* have found the hiding place, Mike has not," he said despondently. "He has gone right past it. Where *is* he?"

Poor Mike felt he was in one of his unpleasant dreams in which he was being followed and there was no way of escape. He had run around the huge rock with Jack and Paul close behind when, all of a sudden, they had disappeared. Knowing they would not have made for the lake, he turned to the right hoping to spot them, only to find his way blocked by an enormous boulder.

He retreated and, almost in a panic as he could hear approaching footsteps and see a ray of light flashing, tried another route, now having to use his torch as the rocks prevented the moonlight shining on the ground ahead. He staggered onwards, in his haste tripping over a large stone. Picking himself up, he tried to calm down by taking deep breaths.

He listened. Except for the sound of his own breathing there was only an uncanny silence. His imagination began to run riot as he became convinced there was somebody behind him. He spun round ready to yell, but all he saw were more rocks and shadows. Again he turned, his mouth open with fear. Where were the people following him? Why didn't they make a sound? And *where* were Jack and Paul?

The silence and stillness were scary. Wondering what on earth to do and feeling completely lost, Mike decided to remain where he was for a while. If he moved, he would give away his position. He glanced around, hoping to spot the hiding place that he had already used twice although, of course, in the dim light there was no way he could see it.

Then he heard a muffled cough – a man's cough. The man was obviously nearby – but where, exactly? In front? To one side? Or, more worryingly, behind?

Straining his eyes as he peered through the darkness, Mike could only make out the dim outlines of the rocks blocking out the light from the moon. He stiffened as he suddenly heard a footstep, followed by another. He spun round, seeing nobody. Did the man know he was standing there, frightened? Perhaps the man was slowly creeping up on him, getting ready to pounce. It was like a nightmare – except that it was really happening so he couldn't escape by waking up.

Mike crouched down, hoping that whoever was approaching would pass by. His hopes were dashed as a torch was switched on and flashed around the boulders. Mike panicked. Instead of remaining completely still where he was, he began to run and was immediately spotted!

Giving a nasty yell of satisfaction, the man dashed after him. Having to use his torch, Mike kept dodging around boulders to avoid being picked out by the bright light from the man's torch. Not having the slightest idea where he was, he kept stumbling onwards and onwards, all the time hearing the shouting from his pursuer growing louder and closer.

Mike did not dare turn to see who was following him. He stumbled round more corners, tripped over a large stone and dodged between two boulders, before coming to a halt seemingly surrounded by dark, menacing rocks, just as in his nightmare!

In despair, he scrambled on to the lowest of them, grazing his knee as he hurried to the other side, and twisting his ankle as he leapt down onto the rough ground. Hobbling along, he prayed that the man following hadn't seen him climbing over the rock. Feeling a little relieved, he tucked his torch into his belt as there was sufficient moonlight now to guide him. He began to breathe more easily when, to his dismay, something again blocked his way. His heart almost missed a beat as the something moved! Two huge, strong arms reached out and grabbed hold of the terrified boy who let out a loud cry as he struggled violently.

But it was no use. Mike had been captured!

Mike Is Held Prisoner

Horrified, Jack and Paul heard Mike's anguished yell. "Mike has either hurt himself or has been caught," said Jack, feeling very concerned. "I must discover what has happened. Stay here, but don't worry – I'll make sure I don't get caught."

Cautiously, Jack emerged from between the boulders and looked around. The shadows were still – there was no sign of movement anywhere. Then, some distance away, he heard Mike protesting and a man shouting. With a sinking feeling in his stomach, he knew there was no doubt about it. Mike had been captured.

Jack climbed onto a flat boulder in the shadow of a larger one, confident he could not be seen. At once he spotted a dim, moving light near the mountains, well away from where he was. Could that be Mike and his captor? Trying to work out where they were making for, Jack guessed they were near the derelict farmhouse. Longing to follow, he knew it would be folly to do so as someone else was out there, and that somebody was not showing a light so could be anywhere, even nearby.

At this thought Jack jumped down off the rock. It became clear that the most important thing was to take Prince Paul back to the safety of the platform. He knew only too well how terrible it would be if a Prince of Baronia were captured, as those who held him could demand almost any ransom. Hating the idea of seeming to abandon Mike, Jack crept back to where Paul was hiding and called him. At once a head poked out between the two boulders.

"Mike has been caught," stated Jack in a quiet, subdued tone. "I think I know where he's being taken but we daren't do anything right now in the dark, especially as somebody else is around. We must return to our platform. This time, we must keep well to the right of the waterfall."

The two weary boys splashed through the stream leading from the falls to the lake, the cold water helping to keep them awake. Constantly peering all round, Jack slowly led the way up the gravelly mountainside. He tried to keep in the shadow of the rocks, not daring to use his torch. It was slow going as they had to make certain they were placing their feet on something solid. Every so often, they paused to look back down in the valley, which looked deserted, although they knew only too well that it wasn't.

It took ages before they reached their platform. Before clambering on to it, Jack quietly called out to the girls he assumed were in the passage so as not to frighten them by suddenly appearing. However, they were outside, huddled together in fear.

"Mike's been caught, hasn't he?" wailed Nora, tears running down her face.

"We thought you would *all* be caught because we saw flashes in the darkness and somebody came down the mountain," said Peggy. "We couldn't warn you because whoever it was passed close to here instead of going to the bottom. We were terrified he'd discover our hiding place."

"He had obviously seen you three so signalled to the person hiding in the old farmhouse," added Nora through her tears.

"It was probably Nikitu. He had planned to meet Konstantin on the mountain," said Jack remembering what was said in the cottage. "As you say, he must have spotted us in the moonlight. Gosh, I hope he didn't notice what we were doing."

"I tried to see what was happening through the field glasses," said Peggy, "but they don't work very well in the dark."

"You all disappeared for a while until somebody used a torch and we saw Mike being pushed along," sniffed Nora. "I'm sure he was being led to where the signalling first came from. We can't just go to sleep. We've got to rescue him."

"We cannot do anything in the dark," said Jack decisively. "I want to rescue Mike as much as you do, but it would be silly to go down there now. There's another person lurking in the valley – possibly more than one – and we would probably end up getting captured ourselves, especially as we're so tired."

"Oh no, look, there is another light, look!" cried Paul who had almost fallen asleep. "On the other side of the lake. There *is* a third person down there."

"The light's moving away," said Jack, gazing at the beam being switched on and off. "It'll be the second man. He must be near the cottage and I bet he's shining his torch to mislead us like the man on the mountain."

Paul scowled, saying nothing as he was feeling too tired. Jack insisted they should get some sleep and decide how to rescue Mike in the morning. Back to their beds they went, Nora still sobbing quietly despite Jack's assurances that they would attempt to find Mike the next day. She drifted off to sleep wondering what her twin brother was doing.

When he was captured, Mike tried to struggle and kick, but had to give up as his extremely strong captor held him in a vice-like grip. The boy continued to yell and protest, hoping the others would be able to work out where he was being taken. The man addressed him in Baronian even though Mike was shouting in English, all the time being pushed towards the derelict farmhouse at the foot of the towering mountain.

Suddenly Mike nearly jumped out of his skin as a second shadowy form emerged. He spoke briefly before shining his torch on Mike's face. Seeing a boy, he uttered a loud exclamation of surprise then melted away into the darkness once again. Mike stumbled along until, eventually, a long dark object barred the way. It was a stone wall. He was led alongside it and around a corner where he saw the outline of the farmhouse. Surprisingly, he was forced past it to another building, eerily silhouetted against the dark mountainside. The man unlocked a door with a huge key and roughly thrust Mike inside, letting go of him.

He shouted some questions and was clearly annoyed that Mike could not understand him. Shaking his head, he uttered some incomprehensible instructions, pointing to the ground, before leaving. With a sinking

feeling in his stomach, Mike heard the door being locked and a bar being slid across it. Wondering where he was as the room was quite smelly, he realised he still had his torch tucked into his belt. He took it out and shone the light around. The light felt on stone walls with a wooden upper section. Here and there were piles of hay. It was clearly an old barn, just like Uncle Henry's. Surprisingly, the lock on the door seemed fairly new, unlike the door itself.

A rickety ladder led to an upper storey, although

Mike was too weary to consider exploring. In the roof was a small, cobweb-covered skylight. Accepting the fact he could not escape and feeling tired and miserable, he piled up some of the hay, making himself a bed. So exhausted was he that in no time he was fast asleep.

All five children had a restless night in the Secret Valley as their beds were far from comfortable. Had they not been so tired, they would have had little in the way of sleep. They were suddenly awakened quite early in the morning by the sound of an aeroplane skimming the mountain tops before, as on previous occasions, circling the valley. Paul and the girls were about to rush out on to the platform when Jack yelled at them.

"Keep down! Don't for goodness' sake let yourselves be seen by the watchers in the valley!" he cried. "All is lost if our hiding place is discovered. Keep as low a possible on the platform and wave frantically when the plane returns."

All of a sudden Paul let out a yell of delight before being roughly pulled down by Peggy. "It's the secret plane! I thought it sounded different!" he shouted. "Look how it goes close to the mountains and turns at the last moment. Please, please, come over here and find us, Captain Arnold, if you're flying it."

It was, indeed, the secret plane making its incredible manoeuvres. At times it seemed to hover over parts of the valley. Then it purred as it flew from one side to the other, narrowly missing the threatening mountainsides by zooming sharply upwards. It was a remarkable sight! The children watched in awe as it flew around the valley once again but, alas, without hovering over the platform.

151

"*Please* see the SOS stones," begged Nora, waving wildly. "Please rescue us."

Whether or not the letters had been noticed was unclear, as the plane returned over the mountains to its base. Looking down at the grassy clearing, the children admired the night's work – the letters SOS could be clearly read. A delighted Jack took hold of the field glasses and focused on the derelict farmhouse where he assumed Mike was being held.

He suddenly stiffened. A figure was dodging from rock to rock, obviously trying to conceal his progress. For a short time the man disappeared from view, then there he was, close to the old farmhouse. While Peggy prepared some breakfast, Jack kept the glasses trained on him and on the farmhouse, reporting what he saw. In due course, a different man appeared – clearly the huge ape-like one – who was bending low, like the first, as he disappeared behind the rocks and boulders.

"It looks as though the man who captured Mike is being replaced by another person," observed Jack. "The farmhouse doesn't look a secure place to keep a prisoner, so I hope Mike wasn't tied up all night."

"Jack, let's try to rescue him as soon as we've eaten," pleaded Nora, her face pale with worry.

"Don't worry, I intend to," said Jack. "First I want to try to see where the man is making for. We can eat out here as long as we don't stand up. Afterwards we can freshen up in the waterfall."

While he ate, Jack kept sweeping the valley with the field glasses. From time to time the man disappeared from view, ending up quite close to the cottage. It meant there were two people unaccounted for whom Jack was convinced were still in the valley.

"They're probably hiding near the cottage," said Jack, "but I still refuse to believe they're in the underground room."

"Perhaps they're deliberately hiding near the cottage, hoping they'll catch anyone who approaches it," suggested Peggy.

"You're almost certainly right," agreed Jack. "Approaching the cottage would be walking into a trap. Well, I'm convinced there's only one person on guard at the farmhouse so let's hurry and finish eating."

The meal over, they had a quick splash in the waterfall which really woke them up. While they dried themselves, Jack outlined his plan.

"We'll make our way to a spot just above the farmhouse," he explained. "There seems to be a sort of rocky barrier all the way round which we can keep behind. Once there, you act as lookouts while I go down to the building to see how we might rescue Mike. I'll wave if I need help. Bring a jersey to wave in case you see anyone coming."

The four cautiously wended their way along the uneven mountainside, keeping a lookout for any movement in the valley below. Everything was still. Having to make a few detours to avoid being visible to anyone watching, they eventually found themselves above the farmhouse, noticing for the first time the old barn and various outhouses.

"This is going to be more complicated than I thought," said Jack, gazing down. "I assumed Mike was in the farmhouse, although he could be in any of those buildings except the one with no roof."

"Look, someone's come out of the farmhouse," said Nora urgently. "He's going over to one of the other buildings."

"It looks like he's carrying food," declared Peggy looking through the glasses. "Could he be going to Mike?"

"Yes, I bet he is," replied Jack, looking pleased. "So now we know where Mike is being held prisoner – in that barn. Yes, look. It's the man with the brown beard. His name's Georgi."

Putting down the tray, Georgi slid aside the stout wooden bar which helped keep the door securely closed before producing a large key and unlocking the door. He picked up the tray and went inside. Nothing happened for a couple of minutes, then he came out, locked the door, slid back the bar and returned to the farmhouse.

Jack waited a while before announcing his intention of going down to the barn. After giving a reminder to wave Peggy's jersey if they saw anyone coming, he slithered down the mountainside, trying to keep in the shelter of tall rocks. The others watched him safely reach the barn, pause for a few moments, and then go round the back out of sight. He had been gone for some time when Paul let out a cry.

"There's that woman who is afraid of toads!" he exclaimed. "She is coming towards the farmhouse. Why did we not see her earlier? Wave the jersey, Peggy."

"A fat lot of good that will do now!" retorted Nora pulling a face. "Jack's out of sight so he won't see the jersey. That woman will, though. In any case, she's bound to spot Jack so now there'll be *two* prisoners, not one!"

Jack to the Rescue

How relieved Jack had been to reach the foot of the mountain without anyone in the farmhouse apparently hearing or seeing him! Glancing upwards, he waved to the three friends watching him on the mountainside before very cautiously approaching a gap in the wall he had seen from above. Through this he crept before hurrying towards the end of the barn, keeping the building between him and the old house.

The lower part of the barn was constructed of stone like the farmhouse; the upper part was built of timber and what seemed to be thatch. Various shrubs and bushes grew untidily alongside. There were no windows apart from the skylight in the roof and, not surprisingly, no gaps anywhere in the solid walls.

At the far corner grew a small, leafy tree – an unusual sight in the Secret Valley. Jack crept warily round it to survey the side of the barn. Standing back a short way to look up at the roof, he spotted the small window, reminding him of the one in the barn on his grandfather's farm. Now he had to be extra careful as he made his way along the side wall, as he knew he would soon be visible to anyone watching from the farmhouse.

"It's no use going any further," he said to himself. "I know what's round the next corner – the door, and that is in full view of the farmhouse. Whoever's in the house must keep watching the mountainside for any sign of us. That leaves only the small window in the roof as a way in. Now, *how* can I reach it?"

He managed to find a few footholds in the stone wall, but they were insufficient to allow him to reach the roof. Annoyed, he looked around for something to help him climb. There was nothing. The people who lived in the farmhouse must have taken their tools with them when they abandoned the valley. As he glanced back at the barn, his gaze fell on the tree in the corner.

"Of course, the tree! Why didn't I think of it before?" he thought angrily. "It looks as though it's as high as the roof. I must get to that window and see if Mike is in the barn. I'm sure he is but I daren't call his name."

He hurried back to the tree, delighted to find the upper branches were overhanging the roof. Listening for any sounds, he shinned up it and carefully lowered himself on to the roof. The thatch remained firm, although the old timbers sagged a little under his weight. Only too well aware he could now be seen by anyone watching from the mountainside, he glanced up to where he supposed Paul and the girls were and immediately received a shock. Peggy's jersey was being waved!

Jack at once lay flat. The jersey meant there was someone nearby. But where? Was it the man from the farmhouse or was somebody else approaching? He scanned the mountainside in case there was somebody up there – someone who could not fail to spot him on the roof of the barn. He could not, however, detect any movement, not even from the other children who were obviously watching.

Wriggling up to the ridge of the roof, he slowly peered over, just in time to see Kristina come through the gap in the stone wall, bent over as though trying to avoid being noticed. "She's clearly wary of being seen by us," thought Jack with a grin as he watched her hurry across the yard to the farmhouse door, calling to Georgi. The door opened and in she went, closing it behind her. Jack was now faced with a dilemma. A short way down the other side of the roof was the window. Should he make for it now and risk being noticed, or should he wait and risk being able to do nothing if Georgi or Kristina entered the barn?

Deciding on the former line of action, Jack crawled across the roof then, with a little difficulty, down to the window. Annoyingly, it was covered with grime on the outside and cobwebs on the inside. There was no way he could see through it into the barn!

Jack inspected the frame, which seemed to be weak and out of line in places. Taking out his pocket knife, he began to carve a chunk out of the rotten wood, causing the frame to sag and setting the window at a strange angle. Soon there was a sizeable gap. Realising that anyone in the room could not fail to be aware of his presence, he called softly through the gap.

"Mike, are you there?" he called, dreading there would be no reply. He was overjoyed to hear Mike's voice shouting up to him.

"Jack, it's you up there! Thank goodness. I wondered what on earth was going on up there on the roof. How did you get there? That window doesn't open, but you can break it."

"Listen, Mike," replied Jack having a quick look round what he could see of the valley. "There's no time to lose. Kristina is in the farmhouse with the man Georgi. I'm going to try to break the frame, then the window should collapse, so keep clear because of falling glass. If I suddenly stop, it will mean I've spotted someone. While I'm doing this, you must think of a way of climbing up to the window."

"OK, but please hurry, Jack," called Mike moving away. "It's awful in here." He looked around, wondering if the rickety old ladder would hold his weight. To his annoyance, he realised it would not actually reach the window. It did, however, reach the small upper storey, no doubt being in the barn for that very purpose. There was nothing else which he could stand on and there were certainly no footholds in the wall.

Jack continued scraping away with his knife until three sides of the frame had been almost destroyed. Checking that nobody had left the farmhouse and shielding his face from flying glass, he put pressure on the old skylight with his foot and, with a loud crack, it gave way, falling down into the barn where the glass shattered into pieces.

At once Jack sprawled flat, looking across to the farmhouse. Had anyone heard the breaking glass? Nobody appeared, so he crawled to the gaping hole where the window had been and peered through. A forlorn Mike was looking up at him, still desperately trying to think of a way to reach the large gap in the roof.

"The ladder only reaches as far as the upper storey,

not the roof," he shouted. "And the upper storey is just that bit too far away for me to reach out to you from it."

Clicking his tongue in exasperation, Jack peered down into the barn to see the position of the upper storey. An idea quickly entered his head. "I've thought of a grand plan, Mike," he called. "First of all, kick the broken glass out of the way. When you've done that, climb up the ladder to the higher level. Don't, for goodness' sake, knock the ladder over, and check each rung before you put your weight on it. At least one is bound to be rotten, so avoid treading on the middle of the rungs."

Mike made the ladder as firm as possible before slowly climbing up, testing each rung carefully before allowing it to take his weight. Two rungs did give way, but the others remained secure despite creaking ominously. He soon managed to scramble on to the upper section of the barn, making certain not to knock the ladder.

"So near and yet so far!" he exclaimed in annoyance, observing the short distance between where he was and the window frame. "It's no use! There's no way I can get to you even though you're so close."

"You've only heard part of my plan," shouted Jack reassuringly. "Listen carefully as this next bit is going to be very, very tricky. Pull up the ladder – don't let it drop, whatever you do!"

It was not easy to carry out this instruction, as the wooden ladder was fairly heavy and extremely awkward to handle. With some difficulty, Mike managed to raise it to the upper floor where he was standing.

"I've got it up here, Jack," he puffed. "What now?

What's your plan?"

"Pass one end up to me so I can rest it safely against the roof timber," said Jack. "It's vital you check that your end is wedged firmly up against something so it won't slip because you'll then have to try to climb up to the roof. You'll only manage to do so if your end of the ladder is near the edge of whatever you're standing on, or the angle will be wrong and your back won't clear the roof."

Mike looked aghast. This was certainly not going to be an easy task! Cautiously he passed one end of the ladder to Jack, who rested it against one of the strong roof beams now exposed by the broken and rotted window frame. Mike pushed aside wisps of straw to try to find a firm place to rest his end of the ladder. However, he looked in vain. The floorboards of the upper storey were fairly rotten, with gaps near the edge.

In despair he placed the ladder in the gaps, expecting them to grow only larger. Little shreds of wood tore from a main beam, but to Mike's delight the ladder seemed to be firmly held. He looked up to Jack, realising what he had to do now was both difficult and dangerous.

With Jack holding the ladder firmly and peering down anxiously, Mike cautiously tried the first rung. The ladder wobbled a bit without actually moving. Slowly he took a second step, then a third, his eyes fixed on Jack. Feeling far from stable, the ladder creaked and shook with each step he took. Suddenly he let out a cry as his foot slipped through the ladder. He had reached one of the broken rungs!

He regained his composure as, his throat dry, he

swallowed and hesitatingly searched for the next rungs
with each foot in turn. He was just over halfway up when
he made a terrible mistake. He glanced down! The sight

of the stone floor far below made him freeze in horror and feel quite sick.

"Jack, it's no good, I'm g... g... going to fall," he stuttered, beginning to shake. "The ladder's giving way."

"Get a grip on yourself, Mike!" ordered Jack firmly. "Hold tight and look up at me. That's right. I am holding the ladder and it is certainly not giving way. Now keep looking at me and take a deep breath. Don't give up now, please, Mike. You're almost there. Carry on as soon as you're ready."

Poor Mike found himself sweating and trembling as he fixed his gaze on Jack. Gritting his teeth, he climbed up one more rung, now feeling the ladder begin to bend under his weight. Taking another deep breath, he inched his way upwards, dreading that the ladder would give way. Still frightened, he gripped both sides, not daring to take hold of Jack's hand which was now outstretched. Fortunately, he remembered the second broken rung and, with difficulty, placed his foot on the next one.

"I'll be ready to grab hold of you," said Jack calmly as Mike was about to emerge through the hole. "Come on, you can do it. Another couple of rungs and you're out."

Once again Mike climbed upwards. Realising he was almost on the roof gave him some confidence. But unfortunately, two things happened that completely destroyed that confidence. Firstly, he was just about to pull himself through the hole when he heard a frightening sound. It was the heavy key being turned in the lock of the barn door. In a panic he thrust his arms upwards when there came an even more alarming sound. The ladder cracked loudly before splitting in two and crashing down to the floor below.

Escape – and Capture!

What a commotion there was! As the ladder collapsed, a terrified Mike just managed to grip the timbers around the broken window frame, his legs dangling, while a concerned Jack was shouting at him to haul himself higher so he could grab him. Inside, the barn echoed with furious yells as Georgi and Kristina saw their prisoner on the verge of escaping.

"Higher, higher," shouted Jack as Mike desperately attempted to raise his body through the framework, dreading one of the enemy would seize his legs and pull him back down. Jack took hold of Mike's arms, making him wince as he painfully rested a knee on the bare timber. Eventually Mike was pulled free and he flopped down on the sloping thatch, quite exhausted.

"I know you're puffed but follow me, we haven't a moment to lose!" cried Jack. "Whoever entered the barn will run outside and catch us as we climb down. Come on, we've go to scramble over to the corner of the roof."

In a daze, poor Mike clambered over the roof and crawled towards Jack who was holding a branch, praying the enemy would not be below, ready to pounce. He began to climb down. Almost at once, his fears were realised as he heard footsteps running towards him. *Now* what could he do?

On the mountainside, Paul and the girls could not believe their eyes when they saw Jack climb up on the roof, crossing it as stealthily as a cat. As he stopped by the skylight, they dreaded the man or woman would leave the farmhouse and spot him.

"Whatever's he doing?" asked Nora, watching Jack hacking away at the rotten frame. "He can't rescue Mike through the window. It's much too high and he hasn't got a rope."

"I bet Jack has a plan," said Peggy, guessing correctly. "While I keep an eye on the farmhouse door, you two watch for anyone approaching. Remember, there are others in the valley. Look for sudden movements between rocks. And we'd better hide too."

They retreated behind some rocks, around which they cautiously peered. Nora and Paul surveyed the valley – much of it being visible from their position – although they could see no sign of movement. Peggy's eyes were glued to the farmhouse door which she was certain would be opened any moment.

Gazing at the wall at the rear of the farmhouse, Nora suddenly gave a stifled cry. "Look, the man and woman are in the back yard. They're coming round the outbuildings. They'll see Jack on the roof for sure!"

"No, they're at the wrong angle," declared Peggy, annoyed she had not considered the farmhouse would have more than one door.

"There's Mike!" cried Paul excitedly, pointing down to the barn. "Jack is trying to pull him out onto the roof."

"Do hurry, Mike and Jack," pleaded Peggy, wishing she could warn the boys of the approaching enemy.

"Those people are definitely going to the barn because the man has taken out that big key. Perhaps Kristina speaks English and wants to question Mike."

Three pairs of eyes were glued to Kristina and Georgi as they approached the barn. Sliding the large bar aside and unlocking the door, the man entered, closely followed by Kristina who slammed the door shut. There was a moment's silence followed by a great commotion. They had spotted Mike escaping!

Then, without warning, Peggy darted off down the mountainside. Paul and Nora looked on in astonishment, wondering whether to follow. They decided to remain where they were in case anyone else appeared.

Such was her haste to reach the barn door that Peggy half slithered, half tumbled down the uneven slope. She had a marvellous plan – if only she could get there in time! Oblivious to the danger, she reached the valley floor, dashed through a gap in the wall and ran as fast as she could across to the barn. Fumbling with the large, unwieldy key, she eventually turned it so that the door was well and truly locked. She struggled with the bar, managing to drag it across so, even if those inside somehow broke the lock or had a spare key, they still could not open the door.

"I do hope Mike has escaped!" thought Peggy as she removed the key before speeding alongside the barn to the tree down which Jack was climbing. It was *her* footsteps he had heard! His look of alarm gave way to one of surprise and delight.

"I've locked the enemy in the barn!" Peggy cried breathlessly, producing the key. "Now they're *our* prisoners."

"Smashing!" exclaimed Jack, a broad grin spreading over his face as he leapt to the ground. He turned to assist Mike. "Hear that, Mike? They're locked in!"

An equally cheerful Mike jumped off his branch, giving a huge smile. "Have you really locked them in? That's super!" he yelled. "I really expected one of them to grab hold of my legs when they saw me dangling in the air."

"Hadn't we better move?" said Peggy, anxiously gazing up at the roof. "They might escape the way you did."

"They can't because the ladder broke," replied Mike, shuddering at the very thought of his experience. "It's a wonder I didn't crash down on the floor with it."

"All the same, we had better return to our platform because we know there are at least two other people about," observed Jack. "Listen. Georgi and Kristina are hammering on the barn door. Anyone nearby will hear them, although hopefully they'll think it's Mike. Let's go and join Nora and Paul. They'll be wondering what on earth's happening."

Before long, the five children were together again. Naturally, Nora and Paul were eager to learn what had happened, but Jack insisted they return to the safety of the platform while they talked. He was inwardly concerned that they would be noticed as they scurried across the mountainside.

"It's almost like coming home," said Nora as they crossed the waterfall. "I feel we've been doing this for ages even though we only entered the Secret Valley yesterday morning."

"Well, *I'd* like something to eat as soon as we're back," declared Mike, feeling hungry as usual. "I had awful bread and cheese. It was horribly stale!"

"I don't suppose the baker calls very often," said Peggy with a grin, dodging the friendly thump Mike aimed at her. "We'll all have something to eat."

"By the way, the sound of a plane woke me up," said Mike, remembering. "Did you wave to it? Did they spot our SOS?"

"It was the secret plane," answered Paul proudly. "Although it left before we could wave, it circled the valley quite slowly at times so there is a good chance *somebody* saw the letters."

All five hoped this was true as they approached their platform. Once there, Peggy gave the barn door key to Paul as a souvenir of the adventure and prepared something to eat while they continued to chat. All the time, Jack kept surveying the valley, puzzled why there was no sign of anyone.

"They're down there somewhere," he said slowly, "lying in wait for us. But *where*? If only there was some movement, some indication of where they are."

"Perhaps they've left the valley," suggested Nora hopefully.

"No, they will not leave until they catch us," answered Jack, shaking his head. "I've an awful feeling they're not far away."

There was a moment's silence as everyone looked down at the peaceful valley. Peggy broke the silence to ask her brother if he had been questioned.

"Yes, but since neither the man who caught me nor

Georgi could speak English, I couldn't answer any questions," replied Mike, helping himself to some food. "Perhaps the woman speaks English. Maybe she was intending to question me."

After they had eaten, Paul casually picked up a torch and wandered off a short way down the passage. As it was another hot day, the others were beginning to wonder if they dared splash about in their waterfall pool when something awful happened!

From either side of the platform came scrambling sounds. The children looked at each other in alarm. Jack was about to order everyone into the passage when, to their horror, two huge, bearded men appeared, leaping

on to the platform. The girls shrieked in terror while Jack and Mike remained speechless at this unexpected and frightening sight.

"So, this is where the lost English children hide!" stated one of the men in a deep voice, a nasty, leering grin on his face. "We have been watching you. How did you enter our valley?"

"We were camping in the other valley, but when we looked for shelter from a storm we ended up here," replied Jack, not liking the look of the men. "Besides, it is not *your* valley."

"Be careful what you say, boy," said the man, a scowl replacing the grin. "We already have one of your party, now we have all five of you, so we will take you to our little cottage – the one you have already visited. We will look after you until the Government of Baronia gives us exactly what we want: all the plans of the new plane. Do as you are told and you won't be hurt. If you disobey – well…" An unpleasant menacing laugh followed.

A fearful Mike recognised the second man as the ape-like one who had caught him the previous night so he kept looking at the ground, hoping he would not be recognised in daylight. Motioning to the five beds, this man said something to his companion in Maldonian, clearly assuming the fifth bed belonged to the boy they had captured.

"You will come with me down the mountain. You boys first, followed by the girls," said the first man. In a sinister voice, he added, "If you do anything foolish, my friend has instructions to throw the girls down the mountain. Do you understand?"

They understood only too well and shivered, as these were obviously strong, ruthless, evil men. With sinking hearts, the four knew there was nothing they could do. Nora began to sob and Jack put his arm round her to comfort her. Mike looked defiant, relieved that neither man realised he was the boy who had been caught the night before.

"Thank goodness they think they still have their prisoner," thought Jack, hoping Paul would not appear, as he would certainly be recognised as a Prince of Baronia. Almost immediately, to his alarm, he heard the prince returning. At once he raised his voice.

"You have no right to take us prisoner!" he shouted, hoping Paul would remain out of sight. "We are on holiday in Baronia. Where is our brother? Why do you treat us like enemies?"

The ape-like man raised a threatening arm, a look of thunder on his face. Jack fell silent, but he had said enough for a frightened Paul to understand something serious was afoot. Paul risked a quick look around the corner and gasped at the sight of the other children leaving the platform followed by a huge man who shouted something about searching for the missing case to his companion.

When he judged it was safe, he looked for the field glasses which he soon found in a corner. He put them to his eyes to watch where the others were being taken, yet to his amazement he could not see anyone.

"They must be there," he reasoned with himself in Baronian. A worrying thought occurred to him. Supposing they were making for the barn? The enemy would realise there was a fifth child somewhere and start searching for him. Wandering a short way down the mountain, he detected a movement below, to the left. There was the huge man he had just seen on the platform. The children also came into view, having been hidden by tall rocks as they descended.

He watched the little procession reach the foot of the mountain, cross the main track and disappear from sight behind thick greenery. Paul guessed they were making for the cottage as the men now believed all the children were captured so they could safely use the ruin. He turned to go back to the platform when he stopped in his tracks. There, coming down the sheer face of the mountain, at what seemed a reckless speed, was someone in uniform He at once recognised that someone – it was the traitor, Konstantin!

Knowing he would be spotted if Konstantin turned, Paul slowly retreated back towards the platform, turned, and yet another shock greeted him. He was sure he saw somebody dodge behind a rock near the platform. Paul was terrified. If he remained where he was, Konstantin would see him; if he moved towards the platform, he risked being caught by whoever was hiding there. Whatever should he do? Trembling, he decided to make for the pool in the waterfall where there was reasonable shelter. If only he could reach it safely.

The frightened prince kept stopping and listening, wondering what the person by the platform was doing. Was he still up there? Or worse, was he lying in wait? Paul felt tears of despair welling up as he took a deep breath, determined not to cry. Instead, he carried on, longing to hear the waterfall's friendly sound.

It was with great relief that he heard the cascading water which meant he was almost there. Just a few more paces... Suddenly he drew in his breath and froze. Passing between two rocks, he saw the man by the platform. And the man, with a flaming red beard, was staring straight down at him!

Ranni and Pilescu Arrive

The man's eyes opened wide in astonishment. "My little lord!" he called in Baronian. "You are safe. But why are you alone? Where are the others?"

"Ranni!" yelled an overjoyed Paul, scrambling up to him. "Oh, Ranni. There are traitors and enemies in this valley. They have taken Jack and the Arnolds prisoners... and the guard Konstantin has just hurried down the mountain... and—"

"Wait, not so fast!" said Ranni, giving his prince a bearlike hug. "First we will go beyond the waterfall. Do not be frightened when we cross the water."

"Frightened!" exclaimed Paul in disgust. "We have sat in pools in the middle of waterfalls!"

Hearing this, Ranni gave a look of great disapproval. He led the way, amazed and proud at the way his prince nimbly leapt across the fall. They scrambled a short way up the mountainside and eased themselves around rugged rocks before reaching a small, flat area. "Before you tell me anything, I shall call Pilescu."

"Pilescu!" exclaimed Paul in disbelief. "Where is he?"

"Nearby," replied Ranni, taking a small radio transmitter from his jacket. He turned and spoke into it. Almost immediately, a familiar figure emerged from behind some large boulders, overjoyed at seeing the prince.

"Pilescu, how did you—" began Paul, but was again interrupted by Ranni.

"We must know what happened to you, and what is this about an enemy and the Arnold children being prisoners?" he asked urgently, glancing at Pilescu who, like himself, was looking concerned. "Sit on this boulder and tell us your story."

The men listened attentively as Paul described the violent storm and were amazed to learn of the passage through the mountain. On hearing about the enemy, they looked at each other in alarm and anger, especially when informed that Konstantin was a traitor. They grinned with delight when Paul produced the barn door key, telling them that there were two prisoners locked inside, but looked grim-faced again on being informed of the capture of the Arnolds.

"Why did the plane not come more often?" asked Paul, finishing his story.

"Ranni and I were delayed setting off from the palace because of storm damage on the runway," explained Pilescu. "Once here, we were horrified to discover your tents near the dangerous mountain ledges above the cabins and assumed you had taken refuge somewhere there. We searched and searched while a plane from the airbase flew over the mountains and valleys. We were so very worried about you. Search parties explored all the caves on our side of the mountain."

"What about our boat?" asked Paul. "Was that not on the other side of the lake?"

175

"No, it was drifting near the island so it appeared you had crossed the lake before the storm arrived," replied Ranni. "Planes did fly over this valley, yet it seemed inconceivable that you should be here. Why did you not wave to them?"

"We could not wave because we were usually hiding from the enemy," explained Paul, looking glum. "Luckily Peggy had the idea of making an SOS signal with stones."

"That was a wonderful idea because Captain and Mrs Arnold spotted the stones and the jersey this morning," said Pilescu. "That provided us with the astounding information that you must be in the valley which is why Ranni and I have climbed over the mountain. However, we did not expect to find an enemy here. As far as you know, how many are there in the valley?"

"Kristina and Georgi are locked in the barn," answered Paul thinking carefully. "Konstantin has just descended the mountain. I heard Nikitu's deep voice when he spoke to the Arnolds and I think it was Ivanu with him. He looks like an ape."

"That's two hopefully still imprisoned, but at least three on the loose," said Ranni looking around. "That underground room you mentioned seems to be their base so that's probably where they are. Point the ruined cottage out to us and, tell me, do these people carry guns?"

"We never saw or heard a gun," said Paul. "It's a good thing, or we would have been all caught earlier. Did you bring yours? And the underground room is in that ruined cottage down there beyond the lake."

"They obviously haven't used guns as they would not risk anyone at the airbase hearing a gunshot in what is supposed to be an uninhabited valley," said Pilescu grimly. "We didn't bring guns as we were unaware of an enemy here. We must catch them before we take you children back."

"How can we leave the valley?" asked Paul. "We can't climb the mountains."

"Be patient, little lord," said Pilescu, patting the prince on the head. "Ranni and I will decide what to do."

"Have you forgotten that *I* am a prince of Baronia?" demanded Paul using his royal voice. "*I* will decide with you. *I* shall help rescue the Arnolds. They rescued me at Spiggy Holes in their country. Now it is *my* turn to help rescue them in the Secret Valley in *my* country."

"Of course you shall decide with us," said Ranni smiling at the indignant prince. "We shall need your help. Now why have the two people locked in the barn not escaped through that window I can see? After all, they are mountaineers."

"It's in an awkward place set in a sloping roof," observed Pilescu. A thought suddenly occurred to him. "Wait, I do believe the traitor Konstantin was present when your SOS signal was reported. Yes, he was. That means he knows we will search the valley. That is why you saw him hurrying down the mountain. He needs to inform the enemy and, having been assigned guard duty on the mountainside today, it was an easy thing to do."

"So they will be expecting us," said Ranni slowly. "Let me look through the field glasses, my little prince.

I want to take a look at that cottage you have told us about."

As soon as Paul handed him the glasses Ranni had a quick look at the farmhouse and the barn before focusing on the ruined cottage near the lake. There was no movement. He looked along the track and stiffened. "Someone is moving towards the mountain near where I found you," he said. "Whoever it is is in a great hurry. It's certainly not Konstantin."

"I have remembered something else," said Paul at once. "As the Arnolds were taken away I heard Ivanu say he would return to look for the case. Let me see."

Ranni bent down while the prince lifted the glasses to his eyes. "Yes, that's Ivanu, the ape-man!" he declared excitedly. "I expect he's coming to our platform."

"Quick, lead us there, little prince," said Pilescu immediately. "He is hurrying as he has heard Konstantin's information. I'll stay in front while you give me directions."

Paul directed the group across the waterfall, describing the platform as they approached it. "It's like a cave, although it really is the exit from the tunnel through the mountain," he explained. "It's behind those rocks ahead. You have to climb onto it."

"We dare not climb in case we're seen," decided Pilescu. "We'll capture him while he's searching. Listen. I can hear loose stones. He must be close."

The sound of falling stones became louder as the man hastily approached. His footsteps on the rough, stony surface suddenly stopped only to be followed by a scrambling sound as he clambered onto the platform.

All went quiet as he entered the cave.

Instructing Paul to remain hidden, Pilescu and Ranni mounted the platform and cautiously approached the passage, keeping to one side as they knew only too well they could be easily seen when silhouetted against the light blue sky. They heard Ivanu rummaging about, then uttering a cry of satisfaction. He had found what he had come for – the precious case!

At once, Ranni darted into the passage, intending to seize his enemy, but his eyes did not adjust to the darkness quickly enough. Ivanu glanced up in time to see the Baronian rushing at him. Using the double advantage of clear vision and the weight of the case, he fought off Ranni's lunges, pushing him against the wall. Ranni grabbed the Ivanu's arm, but had to let go as the man hit him with the heavy case before dashing outside.

Ivanu prepared to leap off the rocky platform, leering smugly at the thought of his successful escape – but he was unaware of Pilescu lying in wait. Pilescu dived at Ivanu's legs, causing him to trip and crash heavily onto the path below, uttering a yell of pain.

At once, the two Baronians grabbed hold of him, now writhing in agony from what appeared to be a broken leg and a badly injured arm. He glared at the men as they questioned him concerning the whereabouts of the Arnolds. After a moment's thought, he pointed to the barn, claiming they were all in there.

"That's not true!" shouted an angry voice as Paul emerged from behind a nearby rock. "You did not take them to the barn."

Ivanu could not believe his eyes. Another child! Surely all five were captured? Gradually it dawned on him who this one was and he stared in disbelief. "Prince Paul of Baronia!"

"That is who I am," replied the prince haughtily. "And you are spying against my country. Where are my friends? Tell me or I shall tread on your leg."

Ranni and Pilescu looked at each other in amazement, managing to suppress smiles as the angry prince approached a furious Ivanu.

"Stop, stop, I will tell," said Ivanu, a look of thunder

on his large, round face. "They are in a hut in the middle of those bushes behind that old cottage down there. You will not be able to rescue them as you will be observed and captured. There are plenty of us in this valley."

"We shall see," said Ranni. "I hope you are telling the truth this time, although I do not believe there are plenty of you in the valley. I shall leave you a mug of water and, as you are behind this tall rock, you will be sheltered from the sun. We'll try not to be away too long!"

Ranni then picked up the case and opened it. He whistled in amazement on seeing the contents and showed them to Pilescu.

"The stolen plans... and... the missing engine part!" exclaimed Pilescu in delight while Ivanu scowled at him. "No wonder this unpleasant man wanted them so badly. The Maldonian government would reward him well for all this."

Closing the case, he hid it between some rocks while Ranni radioed the airbase to inform them what was afoot, although at this stage he did not want anyone else to enter the valley in case it jeopardised the safety of the Arnold children.

Soon they set off down the mountainside, making sure they were hidden at all times behind rocks and boulders. Paul suggested they keep to the right-hand side of the lake as there was more cover there. "Jack and I escaped from the cottage along this side," he explained. "We will reach the track quite close to the ruin."

The three hurried around the lake without seeing anybody and eventually reached the track. Once Paul had indicated the former kitchen with its underground room, Ranni darted silently up to the cottage. He cautiously made his way round it until he spotted two men through a window.

He at once recognised Konstantin, the mountaineering rope still around his waist, his eyes fixed on the mountains, clearly watching for anybody coming over the ridge. Both men were discussing the best way to deliver a ransom demand for the release of the children and how to plead innocence if a search party appeared. The other man, Nikitu, expressed concern that Kristina and Georgi had not returned with the boy, stating he would soon investigate, while Konstantin remarked that Ivanu should also be back by now with the case and its vital contents.

Ranni dashed back to inform Paul and Pilescu of what he had seen and heard. They discussed whether to attempt to capture the two men then rescue the Arnold children or whether to find the children first.

"The problem is that we do not know exactly where the children are or whether releasing them will be a difficult or time-consuming task," reasoned Pilescu. "If Ivanu was telling the truth, they are in a hut somewhere in that mass of greenery over there. Perhaps we should wait until the men separate and capture them one at a time first."

It was while they were deciding what to do with whoever they captured that Nikitu came out and set off towards the lake, presumably making for the barn. There was no sign of Konstantin who was still keeping watch for rescuers coming over the mountain.

Instructing Paul to remain where he was, Ranni and Pilescu crept towards the cottage with the intention of capturing Konstantin and tying him up with the rope he carried. As he was standing near the doorway, the two Baronians had to ease themselves through a window on the far side.

They crept silently through the derelict cottage until they saw the silhouette of their enemy in the doorway. Just as they were about to pounce, Konstantin spun round and reached for something in a pocket.

Ranni and Pilescu froze. That something was a gun!

The Tension Mounts

Konstantin could scarcely believe his eyes. First the children enter the valley and now these two Baronians appear. Uncertain how to react, he decided to fake innocence.

"I wondered who was creeping up on me," he declared, forcing a smile as he lowered the gun. "I was on guard duty when I noticed children in the valley. Although I came down at once, I cannot find them. Perhaps they are hiding."

"I'm sure they won't be hiding," said Ranni calmly, aware that Konstantin was still holding his gun.

"Let us search outside together," suggested Konstantin, not wanting Ranni and Pilescu to separate or see Nikitu returning with Mike. "We'll have a good view by the lake."

They crossed the track, Konstantin wondering if the other two suspected him of wrongdoing. Ranni and Pilescu understood their lives would be in danger if they challenged Konstantin so they accompanied him, hoping for a chance to seize the weapon.

Paul was horrified to see Konstantin with a gun, even though it was not pointed directly at Pilescu and Ranni. Sensing all was not well, he decided to search for the hut in which Ivanu claimed the Arnolds were imprisoned.

He darted across the track to where the bushes, shrubs and weeds had grown undisturbed for several years, but found no trace of a path.

Downhearted, he pushed his way awkwardly through the greenery, thrusting aside branches and foliage. Soon he was surrounded by tall plants and bushes which met overhead to form a kind of living roof. It became very dark and forbidding, and more than a little scary for the young prince. He was beginning to imagine that the ground would open up in front of him to reveal a pit to fall into when he heard voices – familiar ones – and not far away.

With renewed energy he ploughed through more undergrowth until all of a sudden he came upon a stone hut. The voices were coming from behind a stout wooden door with a bar across it, similar to the one on the barn door. At once Paul grabbed hold of the bar and attempted to slide it across while calling out to his friends. The voices stopped when the astonished children realised that Paul was outside.

"Paul, it's you! Great!" called Jack. "Can you get the door open?"

Although the prince pulled, pushed and tugged, the bar refused to budge. Spotting the remains of a log, he picked it up and began knocking the end of the bar with it. At first nothing happened then slowly, very slowly, it moved grudgingly across until it came free. Paul excitedly turned the handle, only to discover another problem. The door was locked!

"It's locked!" he shouted, almost in tears, kicking the door. "It looks like a fairly new lock so it will not break even if I hit it with something."

"Drat, I expect those people fitted a new lock to this door just like on the barn door," moaned Mike. "How did—"

He was interrupted by a loud squeal from Peggy. "A new lock!" she exclaimed. "Of course! The barn door had a new lock. I gave the key to Paul. Do you still have it?"

Realising he did indeed have the key, Paul removed it from his deep pocket, but was fumbling so much with excitement that he could not insert it. Calming down, he took a deep breath before trying again. This time it went in easily. He turned it and the door opened!

The others rushed outside to hug Paul, all talking at once until Jack silenced everyone. "Listen," he said urgently. "We'll lock the door and slide the bar across so it looks like we're still inside. After that we'll move right away."

"I am so pleased I have rescued you as you rescued me at Spiggy Holes," declared Paul, his eyes ablaze. "Listen. I must inform you that Ranni and Pilescu are here in the valley, although I think Konstantin has caught them."

The others stopped, delighted that Ranni and Pilescu were near, but shocked to think they had been caught. Again Jack spoke out. "Not another word until we're away from here," he said firmly, pushing through the dense undergrowth. "We'll find somewhere more suitable to talk."

They emerged near the track, close to a small, grassy

knoll encircled by boulders. Jack led everyone to it where they perched on small rocks. When Paul told his story, the others were horrified to learn that Konstantin possessed a gun.

"He'll shoot Ranni and Pilescu," said Nora beginning to cry. "They know too much."

"No he won't," said Jack, comforting her. "He doesn't know Paul has spoken to them or that we've spotted him with the enemy. He'll probably pretend to be looking for us and act innocently."

"So why did Paul see him holding a gun?" persisted Nora.

"I expect he's concerned that Ranni and Pilescu might suspect him so he has to have the gun ready," guessed Peggy. "I wonder where they are."

"They walked towards this end of the lake," said Paul. "Konstantin will not want my men to spot Nikitu when he returns."

"I'm going to have a recce," announced Mike, clambering on to a ledge from which he could just see the lake. He soon spotted the three men edging their way along and told the others.

"There's an idea coming to me," announced Jack, summing up the situation. "If Konstantin is distracted, either Ranni or Pilescu could seize the gun and capture him. It's up to us to distract him. Follow me, and keep well down."

The children crept towards the far end of the lake where the three men had positioned themselves. When they suddenly spotted Konstantin climbing up on to a boulder, the five fell flat on their stomachs. Luckily the man was concentrating on the other end of the lake so did not see them.

"I bet he's really looking for Ivanu and Nikitu while pretending to look for us," said Peggy.

"You said we had to distract him," said Nora, glancing at Jack. "But *how*? You haven't told us."

"Well, assuming Konstantin remains where he is with Ranni and Pilescu, we'll creep as close as possible without risk to ourselves," explained Jack. "Once there, we'll cause a distraction by throwing stones against a boulder. Konstantin is bound to turn round, so Paul's men can grab him and be free."

The others were delighted at the thought of rescuing the two Baronians, especially Paul who thought the world of them. Jack checked that Konstantin was no longer on his rock before continuing. Progress was slow as they silently approached the three men.

"Pick up a couple of large stones each," instructed Jack as they crouched behind more boulders. "Be ready to pass them to me. Konstantin keeps looking in the same direction so, when the moment looks right, I'm going to hurl the stones in the opposite direction. Mike, you do the same. That should make him jump and turn. But first, we must try to attract the attention of Ranni or Pilescu."

They waited and waited, hardly daring to breathe as they watched Konstantin who was still holding his gun. Paul longed to rush out and hurl the largest stone they had at his country's enemy, but wisely refrained from doing so. Suddenly, they ducked as a figure climbed up onto a rock close by. This time it was Ranni! Shielding his eyes from the sun, he looked all around, hoping to spot Paul. To his utter amazement, who should he see just a short distance away but Jack!

At once Jack raised the stone he was holding, indicating the direction he intended throwing it. Ranni gave a slight nod, discreetly raising a finger to inform the boy to wait a moment. He turned, addressing Pilescu who leapt up on the rock. This time, it was Pilescu who looked astonished to see Jack. The two men turned away, pointing towards the distant waterfall while deliberately making loud references to the children.

This was too much for Konstantin who immediately joined them, gazing in the direction they were indicating and standing on a rock for a better view. Jack knew this was their chance to distract Konstantin. He whispered to Mike, who crept with him towards the unsuspecting man. At a signal from Jack, the boys hurled their stones at a group of boulders behind the men.

Konstantin swung round on hearing the crashing stones, his gun at the ready. The rock being uneven, he began to lose his balance. While he attempted to steady himself, Ranni and Pilescu quickly pounced, knocking him to the ground and causing his gun to fly through the air as they grappled with him. The angry, bewildered man fought desperately, trying to see where his gun had fallen. Spotting it between two nearby boulders, he kicked and lashed out wildly like an enraged animal, his fury knowing no bounds. Half-staggering, half-crawling towards the weapon, he just managed to keep the two men at bay. Soon it was within his grasp.

Despite Ranni holding him by the legs and Pilescu forcing one arm behind his back, he stretched out the fingers of his free hand towards the gun and was on the point of taking hold of it when it was snatched away. Paul had pluckily left his hiding place and grabbed it! He now pointed it at the astonished Konstantin who, clearly recognising the prince, yelled at him not to touch the trigger. Pilescu immediately released the man's arm before calmly taking the gun from the furious prince, who was now calling Konstantin all manner of names.

"*Why* have you done this?" demanded Paul. "Why are you a traitor to our country?"

"Because I am being paid well by the Maldonian government," spluttered Konstantin in Baronian. "And I shall be given a top job in the development of *their* new plane, not just as a guard on the mountain."

"Not now you won't," said Pilescu grimly as the other children appeared. Konstantin blinked, wondering if he was dreaming. Opening his mouth to say something, such was his astonishment that he could utter no words. He made an odd, unpleasant snarling sound as Ranni tied him up with his own mountaineering rope.

"Start shouting and I shall gag you as well," threatened Ranni. "That would be very uncomfortable in this heat."

"That leaves just one more person to find," said Pilescu, checking the gun's safety catch. "See if you can

spot him, Jack."

Jack bounded on to a nearby rock and almost immediately jumped back down, looking shocked. "I hate to tell you this, but there are now *three* people to catch, not one," he announced solemnly. "Nikitu has freed Georgi and Kristina and they're hurrying towards the old cottage!"

"We must move away from here," said Ranni at once. "Although we have the advantage of the gun, we should not ignore the fact that one or more of those three may also possess a weapon. Let's see if we can surprise them."

"I wonder how Nikitu released Georgi and Kristina," said Nora as they left Konstantin.

"Probably the same way Paul rescued us," answered Peggy. "The key I gave Paul fitted the hut door. Ivanu locked us in, so his key would also fit the barn door."

"Keep well back in case they got here before us," instructed Ranni as they drew near to the cottage. "We'll wait here a moment."

No sooner had he uttered these words than three figures crossed the track by the old cottage. Nikitu's deep voice was heard calling for Ivanu as they went in. In next to no time he appeared outside again, striding through the overgrown garden towards the dense greenery.

"He's going to the hut," whispered Nora. "Won't he get a shock!"

"Let us lock him inside," said Paul, his eyes ablaze. "Like he made my friends prisoners."

"I intend to do just that," stated Pilescu, keeping a

lookout in case Georgi or Kristina appeared. "Stay with Ranni, everyone. Paul, please give the key to me."

"You'll need to slide a wooden bar across the door too," said Mike urgently as Paul handed over the key, "or he'll simply unlock the door from the inside with his own key."

Pilescu dashed across the track and pushed his way through the bushes, trying to make as little noise as possible. He could hear the sound of the bar being awkwardly slid across the door – not that he knew what it was until he peered between some large leaves. Watching Nikitu produce a key from his pocket, he approached, the gun at the ready.

"Good day to you," he called politely in Baronian.

Nikitu swiftly turned round and was astonished to see Pilescu. "Who are you? Why are you here? What do you want?" he demanded.

"All questions will be answered in good time," replied Pilescu. "Please continue unlocking the door."

At first Nikitu hesitated then, observing the gun being slowly raised, he inserted the key and turned it.

"Leave the key in the lock and enter," instructed Pilescu.

Nikitu pulled open the door and entered, expecting to find four frightened children inside. A look of incredulity crossed his face on finding the building empty. Had he not locked the children in here earlier? And had the key not left his possession? Turning for an explanation he found the door being closed.

His reaction was swift. He hurled his large body against the door with all his might. The door hit Pilescu, catching him off guard and knocking him off balance. Nikitu grabbed the hand holding the gun in an attempt to make Pilescu drop the weapon. The two strong men struggled violently with each other. Suddenly Nikitu gave Pilescu a vicious kick, causing him to double up in pain. This was followed by a punch, sending the gun flying to the end of the hut.

With a triumphant look on his face, Nikitu ran to retrieve it.

The End of the Adventure

Quickly assessing the situation, Pilescu slammed the door shut, locked it and began sliding the wooden bar across. It was almost in place when there was a loud report from inside the hut as Nikitu fired the gun at the lock. It splintered but did not break while Pilescu hurriedly retreated through the dense undergrowth.

As he reached the track, he spotted a concerned Ranni who had naturally heard the shot. Ranni at once warned him to remain still. He soon saw why. Georgi and Kristina were leaving the cottage, amazingly not showing any surprise at the sound of the gunshot. Georgi crossed the track while Kristina strode purposefully towards the waterfall. Pilescu swiftly joined the others, informing them what had happened.

"Are you all right?" asked Paul, looking at Pilescu's bruises. Then he gleefully added, "We thought you had shot Nikitu. At least he is a prisoner even if he does have the gun."

"Why only one shot?" asked Mike. "And why didn't Georgi and Kristina go to investigate?"

"I expect they were in the underground room so didn't hear it," replied Jack. "But you're right about the single shot. Why only one?"

"Because there was just one bullet," explained

Pilescu. "Now we have to find a way of catching Georgi and Kristina."

"I'm going to radio the base to inform them what is happening," decided Ranni, producing his transmitter.

While Ranni radioed the base, Pilescu and the children peeped around the boulders at Georgi, who was clearly searching for something or someone. He kept bending down and peering round rocks, now and then leaping up on to one to see further.

"I bet he's looking for Mike," said Nora. "He knows Mike is somewhere around, but believes the rest of us are shut up in the hut."

"It's not going to be easy to catch him," observed Pilescu as Ranni finished transmitting. "He keeps changing direction so it will be difficult, if not impossible, to creep up on him."

"We cannot risk letting him find Konstantin or he will free him," warned Ranni. "I notice he is gradually heading in Konstantin's direction. We'll have to prepare to run at him – and hope he does not have a weapon."

"I know how you can catch him!" declared Mike excitedly. Everyone looked at him for an explanation. "If you – Ranni and Pilescu – find hiding places behind two close-together boulders, I can approach Georgi, who will see me and chase me while I lead him to where you're hiding."

The two Baronians looked at each other for a moment before replying. "I don't like you being exposed to danger," said Ranni. "That man Georgi must be desperate to have revenge on you for locking him in."

"But you and Pilescu will be nearby," protested Mike,

trying not to raise his voice.

"It is an excellent idea – and we will be close by," pointed out Pilescu to his friend.

"Right, we'll do it," agreed Ranni decisively. "He'll certainly chase you without thinking first. You others stay out of sight while Pilescu and I find hiding places. If he produces a gun, Mike – which I doubt or he would have used it when he chased Jack and Paul around the lake – stop immediately."

There was no difficulty finding suitable boulders on either side of what looked like a fairly overgrown path. Pilescu removed a length of rope from around his waist, ready to tie up Georgi if they caught him successfully.

"We're ready, Mike," he called. "As soon as we jump at Georgi, hide."

His heart pounding, Mike crept to where he knew Georgi was and, trembling slightly, climbed on to a flat boulder. There was Georgi, nearby, stroking his brown beard while peering across the lake. The man moved to gaze towards the waterfall and landslide, finally turning right round. He immediately spotted Mike.

His eyes ablaze, and spluttering a bellow of fury, the enraged Georgi shot towards Mike like an arrow from a bow. The boy leapt off the boulder, turned on his heels and fled, remembering his terrifying run during the night. At least this time he knew where he was going. Round a boulder he flew, between two large rocks and along the overgrown path... and, suddenly, he tripped!

Picking himself up, he breathlessly set off again, hearing Georgi's yells perilously close behind. Mike now began to feel afraid as he had hurt his ankle and was not moving very quickly. Between more boulders he half-stumbled, half-limped, expecting to be grabbed any moment. The footsteps behind were now very loud indeed, as was the shouting. Unable to run, he staggered past two more boulders convinced he was about to collapse. Terrified, he turned to face Georgi.

What a relief! Instead of Georgi bearing down on him as he had expected, there was the man on the ground grappling with Ranni and Pilescu. Without realising it, Mike had passed the boulders where the Baronians were hiding! Taken completely by surprise, the struggling Georgi was no match for the two strong men who wasted no time in pinning him down and tying him up.

The other children emerged from their hiding place,

cheering wildly to see another of the enemy bound hand and foot. Like Konstantin, Georgi was utterly bewildered by the events. He made a few angry utterances, fiercely scowling at everybody – especially at poor Mike who had twice caused him to be trapped.

Jack, who had climbed on to a rock to look for Kristina, spotted her returning. Grinning, he called to Ranni and Pilescu. "Guess who's coming? I hope you've enough rope for one more. Our Secret Valley is becoming quite cluttered with prisoners!"

Before either man could reply, everyone fell silent as a hauntingly purring sound was heard above the mountains. To the children's delight, a plane appeared – and not just an ordinary one! It was the secret plane,

gleaming blue and silver and flashing as the sun's rays struck its satin-like surface. At once Ranni ran out on to the track, ignoring the approaching woman, and waved wildly, instructing the children to remain exactly where they were.

The beautiful, sleek plane hovered over the track then turned a full circle before landing gently and bumping its way towards the children watching it in wonder and admiration. Even Prince Paul was speechless. No sooner had it come to a standstill than the door opened and six smart uniformed guards emerged. While they were immediately briefed by Ranni and Pilescu, two more people came through the doorway. Captain and Mrs Arnold!

What an emotional scene it was, with hugs and kisses all round and everybody talking at once! Finally Captain Arnold addressed the children. "You can tell us everything when we are back at the base, as others will also want to hear what seems to be an incredible story," he said. "We only have a brief outline based on what Ranni transmitted. What he said sounded unbelievable and yet, here you are, in the deserted valley."

"The *Secret* Valley!" corrected Paul at once. He looked round triumphantly. "I said we'd find the spies here and we did! What's more, you were wrong, Mike. It looks like I *am* going to have a ride in the secret plane. And so are all of you."

"What's the matter with your leg, Mike?" asked an anxious Mrs Arnold, noticing her son limping.

"Nothing much," replied Mike casually. "I was being chased by an enemy. Guess what! Paul rescued us from a hut where we were imprisoned."

Captain and Mrs Arnold looked at each other in amazement. The things these children got up to! But they inwardly admitted that they always wanted their children to be adventurous.

"I say! We've forgotten about Kristina!" announced Jack, to the further surprise of Captain and Mrs Arnold. "Ranni. Pilescu. Where is Kristina?"

Everyone turned to look, including the surprised guards. There was no sign of her. Pilescu addressed the guards, pointing in the direction where Kristina had last been seen, adding she was almost certainly hiding nearby. The guards spread out, carefully watching for the least sign of movement, guessing she would have moved away from the track.

The children watched, longing for Kristina to be found so that they would leave the Secret Valley knowing all the enemy were safely captured. However, nothing stirred except the guards moving slowly onwards. Captain Arnold was on the point of telling the children to board the plane when there was a loud, piercing scream. There, scrambling onto a boulder, was Kristina! Then, giving another equally loud scream, she tumbled off it while several small creatures jumped up at her.

At this, Paul dissolved into such a fit of giggles that he also tumbled and rolled on the ground. A very concerned Mrs Arnold hurried over to him, astonished as tears of uncontrollable laughter ran down his cheeks. "It... h... h... happened!" he struggled to say. "The t... t... toads jumped at her and m... m... made her f... f...

fall!" More laughter followed, with the other children now joining in much to their parents' bemusement.

The guards ran across to where Kristina had fallen, easily capturing her, and led her over to the derelict cottage. Saying a few words to Ranni and Pilescu, Captain Arnold ushered his wife and the still-giggling children aboard the plane. Only then did they stop laughing as, strapping themselves in, they looked around in awe at all the scientific equipment it carried.

"Just look at all those switches and dials!" exclaimed Paul, longing to get up out of his seat and examine them.

"And all those gauges and screens!" added Mike, scarcely able to believe his eyes. "Gosh, *what* a plane!"

"Oooh, the seats sort of swivel," pointed out Nora, moving a lever by her side. "Aren't they comfortable? I could easily go to sleep."

"Prepare for a bumpy take-off," called Captain Arnold, as the engines gently purred into life. "This is the only plane that can land and take off on rough terrain such as this. Fortunately we have tested it on uneven ground near the base."

"It will seem strange not having to keep dodging behind rocks and hiding from people when we get back," said Nora, sounding very relieved.

"What about Ranni and Pilescu?" asked Paul. "They will join us soon, won't they?"

"Pilescu told me he needs to show the guards where the various prisoners are and some sort of underground room," answered Mrs Arnold. "Not to mention a case containing top secret items. Don't worry, he and Ranni will join us back at the base or the cabins later on."

"You know what? I'm starving!" declared Mike as the plane took off. Everyone laughed, although all the children felt the same. The final part of their adventure had made them all very hungry indeed.

"We didn't thank you for rescuing us, Paul," said Jack leaning across to the prince. "If it wasn't for you we'd probably still be in that hut."

"If it was not for you I would probably still be in the Old House at Spiggy Holes!" replied Paul as the laughter continued. "I say, it was so, so funny when the toads made Kristina fall off the rock."

"He's going to start giggling again," warned Mike, looking out of the window and holding on tight as the plane now swooped up over the valley. "What a view… Oh look, there's the hut where Nikitu is imprisoned."

"Down there are Georgi and Konstantin tied up," pointed out Peggy. "Serves them right."

"Now we're turning I can see the farmhouse and the barn where Mike escaped through the roof," shouted Nora, pointing excitedly.

"And, look, there's Ivanu near our platform!" cried Paul, seeing the man huddled up. "He will not enjoy being taken down the mountain with his bad leg!"

Mrs Arnold shook her head in disbelief at the number of people who seemed to be incapacitated in the valley below. Nevertheless, she looked forward to hearing the children's remarkable accounts of their escapade.

"Goodbye, Secret Valley!" called Mike as they made the short journey over the mountains into their own valley. "You'll soon be peaceful and deserted again."

"It won't really be deserted, because of all the toads!" said Paul, giggling again.

"Do stop giggling, Paul," said Peggy as she thought about everything that had happened. "That was a great adventure we had in the Secret Valley – our second in Baronia!"

"Our best adventures have been in my country," said Paul, still chuckling.

"You would say that!" exclaimed Mike.

"We've been very lucky and had some thrilling times together," said Jack as the plane began its descent. Smiling, he looked round at the others. "One thing's for certain. We'll never ever forget them."